Rewards

THE QUEST OF THE BELLAMY JEWELS

BY

NATALIE BARKAS

FROM AN ORIGINAL FILM PLAY BY

MICHAEL BARRINGER

ABBEY REWARDS
CRESTA HOUSE, LONDON

With grateful thanks to M. B. for valuable suggestions during the making of this book.

THE QUEST OF THE BELLAMY JEWELS

CHAPTER I

A Stowaway and Stolen Jewels

Dusty Bates sat up with a start. He did not know how long he had been asleep or what had roused him. Darkness had fallen and he quickly realized that the *Tilbury Pride* was no longer at sea. She was riding smoothly and the beat of her engines was slow and steady. A swirl of fog drifted to him among the shadows of the deck cargo, and the mournful hoot of a siren came from a passing vessel.

Dusty shivered. Running away to sea was all very well to read about in books, but he was bound to admit that, so far, it had turned out to be uncommonly dull and uncomfortable. He was cramped and cold, he had long ago eaten his small store of food, and pretty soon he'd have to make up his mind what to do next.

Maybe he'd try to find Uncle Hank right away, before the ship came to her moorings. He'd be angry, of course, because this was the second time Dusty had run away from his foster parents in Hull; but Uncle Hank's anger never lasted very long, and Dusty had a sneaking idea that his uncle cared as little for Mr. and Mrs. Huggins as he did himself.

He began to rise cautiously.

The Bellamy Jewels

Suddenly there was a sound of shifting feet followed by a rasping cough. Dusty froze.

"Vhat de ol' man vant to go up-river in dis for, I don' know," complained a slow, foreign-sounding voice.

"Good job for us he does," replied another livelier voice. "We'll be able to pass the stuff on early in the morning, before too many spying eyes are about."

Dusty sank back silently on to his heels, his heart beating fast. Who were these men? What was the "stuff" they were talking about?

"You put the yewels in your kitbag, yaas?"

"Don't talk crazy. Carry 'em ashore with river police all over the place? Not me! That mug Hank Miller has got to take 'em off the way he brought 'em on at Hull. Then, if anything happens, he's for it."

Dusty could hardly believe his ears. Hank Miller, his Uncle Hank, mixed up with a lot of crooks?

"Is good, Tub. Is real good," approved the foreign voice. "Hank take dem ashore. Ve meet him, take de stuff and get de money, an' den ve make de party, yaas?"

"And I'll tell you something else. There won't be no fancy invitation cards for Hank Miller and his pal Squeaky Watts."

"Oh-ho-ho!" rumbled the other. "Not vith a long chalks, no. Vhere are dey now?"

"Down in the fo'c'sle. Can't you hear 'em?"

Dusty listened. Faintly he could hear the whining notes of a concertina. Somehow or other he must warn Uncle Hank. But not yet. He must wait till these men were out of the way. He drew himself closer into his hiding place, all his senses alert.

* * * * * *

Nobody could describe the fo'c'sle of the *Tilbury Pride* as a commodious apartment, and it is unlikely that any-

A Stowaway and Stolen Jewels

body ever did. Such refined and high-sounding phrases seldom fall from the lips of able-bodied seamen. To be accurate, it was long, narrow and dimly lit, and lined on each side with three tiers of dark wooden bunks sufficient to sleep a dozen. Providing that he was impervious to noise, smoke and foul air, a man could roll himself up in a top bunk in its farthest recesses and evade duty for hours at a stretch.

Such a man was Ginger Green, lazy, incompetent, but gifted with a species of low cunning directed exclusively to one end: the avoidance of all but the barest minimum of work. Ginger was the bane of the bosun's life, and in normal times no self-respecting bosun would have retained him. But, nowadays, crews were hard to come by, and so Ginger remained on the strength.

As the *Tilbury Pride* crept slowly up-river Ginger dozed comfortably with a blanket pulled over his head, the strains of the concertina drifting vaguely in and out of his hazy half-dreams. He had climbed into his bunk fully dressed when he came off watch four hours earlier, and he was now due again to report for duty. But the constant booming of fog-horns told him that the fog must be thicker than ever, and Ginger had no difficulty in convincing himself that nobody would miss him for another half-hour. He yawned and stretched himself luxuriously, but with caution. He was well aware that his dilatory habits did not make for popularity with his shipmates, and Hank Miller and Squeaky Watts were no exceptions. When he was good and ready to go on deck he would reveal himself to them. Until then he would lie doggo.

Hank and Squeaky had been buddies for years. Nobody quite knew why, least of all Hank and Squeaky, unless it was that, in a continually changing crew, they alone had remained constant. They had little in common, either in character or tastes. Take music, for instance. As far as Hank was concerned, there was nothing to choose between " God Save the King " and " The Bluebells of Scotland ", in fact, neither could be distinguished by him from " Rock of Ages ", which he had frequently encountered at church services on board ship, or " My Darling Clementine ", which cropped up regularly at every sing-song.

To Squeaky, on the other hand, there was nothing that appealed more than a rollicking tune by a nice brass band. Being a sailor, of course, brass bands did not often come his way. For the same reason Squeaky was unable to indulge his passion by long sessions with the wireless, for the Ixion Steamship Company did not provide such amenities for its crews. But Squeaky was the owner of a dilapidated concertina which he had picked up, as he often wittily remarked, for a song, and all his spare time was spent in coaxing from this ancient relic such tunes of the day as took his fancy.

Just now he was engaged on a rendering of a touching little number which he had heard two nights previously at a music hall in Hull. Lolling on his bunk, his beaky, bird-like head thrown back, and his hands ecstatically pulling and pushing, Squeaky brought his performance to a close with a series of unbelievable discords, and sat up expectantly.

" 'Ow's that, chum?"

" 'Ow's what?" growled Hank, who was sitting on the opposite bunk rearranging his kitbag.

" I'll be your sweetie if you'll only say the word," said Squeaky owlishly.

Hank stared. " You'll be my *what*?" he said indignantly. " Oh, put a sock in it."

A Stowaway and Stolen Jewels

Squeaky sighed. " You got no ear for music," he declared. " None whatever. Wot's eatin' you?"

" It's this 'ere box," said Hank slowly, selecting a cardboard package from his bag and weighing it reflectively in a horny hand. " I dunno as I like the feel of it. Seems to me it's a bit 'eavy like fer terbacco." He raised the package and shook it. " And I never come across no terbacco wot rattled," he added drily.

" Well, let's open it," suggested Squeaky cheerfully. " No 'arm in 'avin' a look-see."

Hank hesitated. Ginger Green, who had listened to this exchange with a mild sort of interest, quietly rolled over and pulled the blanket away from his head. Ginger liked to know what his shipmates were up to. Sometimes he found it quite profitable.

" Go on," urged Squeaky, slipping down from his bunk. " Open it."

Frowning, Hank untied the string and lifted the lid of the box. For a moment he sat speechless, alarm succeeding amazement on his rugged face. Inside, nestling in tissue paper, was a dazzling tangle of brooches, rings, bracelets and necklaces. Diamonds, emeralds, and the deep blue of sapphires sparkled and glittered in the lamp light.

" Well, I'll go ter me tea!" burst out Squeaky in a high-pitched voice.

Hank fixed him with hard accusing eyes.

" A nice thing *you* done for us," he said at last. " 'Ere we are landed with a king's ransom, and 'alf Scotland Yard on the trail, I'll be bound. All because you ain't got no more sense than a wood louse."

" Well, 'ow was I ter know?" complained Squeaky defensively. " That there Tub and Walrus asked me if we'd carry a package aboard at Hull and look after it till we got ashore again."

The Bellamy Jewels

" And wot did you do?" broke in Hank violently. " You made *me* carry it."

" Only because you'd got more room in your kitbag," Squeaky pointed out reasonably, or so he felt.

" And suppose that bag had been searched?"

" Well, it wasn't," returned Squeaky positively. " And don't forget I thought it was only a bit of baccy. Tub told me it was a present for 'is brother, and 'e couldn't trust his-self not to smoke it if he kep' it in 'is own bag."

" Baccy my foot! A nice yarn. There's jewellery and diamonds 'ere worth a fortune. And where did they come from? That's what I'd like to know."

" Who cares?" said Squeaky sulkily, reaching again for his concertina. " It'll be all over to-morrow and we'll get something out of it, maybe."

Hank made an angry gesture. " I don't want 'is dirty money. I've 'alf a mind to go and tell Captain Ford the 'ole story, only——" He broke off suddenly and moved to the foot of the companion. " Wot's that?"

Squeaky stood listening with half-open mouth, his small balloon of confidence abruptly punctured. Ginger Green, in whose mean little mind there had opened a vista of blackmailing ease and power beyond his wildest imaginings, also raised his head and listened.

From down-river, muffled by the fog, came a faint cry.

" Ahoy there! Ship ahoy! Who are you?"

Loud and clear came the answer from the bridge.

" *Tilbury Pride* bound for Blackfriars from Hull. Who are you and what do you want?"

" River Police boat. We are coming up on your stern to board you. Lower a ladder and show a light."

" There you are," said Hank grimly. " Wot did I tell you?"

*   *   *   *   *   *   *   *   *

A Stowaway and Stolen Jewels

The news of the impending arrival of the River Police quickly spread throughout the ship, and to none did it act as a spur more than to Tub Timkins. Tub was playing with fire and he knew it. In choosing Hank and Squeaky as the temporary guardians of the jewels he had relied on Hank's honest reputation and Squeaky's gullibility, and if all had gone well they would have served his purpose admirably. But now he realized astutely that the very qualities for which he had picked them were those most likely to lead to his betrayal. Tub stood in the swirling fog among the deck cargo drawing fiercely on a cigarette, his mind rapidly turning over the possibilities. Beside him lurked the burly Scandinavian Olsen, commonly known as Walrus on account of his sweeping blonde moustache.

Walrus was not remarkable for his intelligence, but he had the shoulders of an ox, there was dynamite in his fists, and, rightly handled, he was a powerful ally. Tub had his own way of handling Walrus.

" Vot ve do now, Tub?" asked Walrus hoarsely.

" Shut up!" snapped Tub. " I'm thinking. In a couple of shakes them coppers'll be poking their noses into everything," he went on, half to himself, " and if they get around to questioning Miller and Watts and searching their gear, our number's up."

Walrus nodded with assumed wisdom. So long as nobody expected him to do the thinking, he was ready to fall in with any plan within reason, and Tub was never short of ideas.

" The first thing to do," decided Tub swiftly, " is to get the stuff hidden." He stamped out his cigarette and took a quick look round. " Come on down to the fo'c'sle."

As the two men disappeared down the companion to the men's quarters, a small dishevelled figure crept through the mist from the shelter of the deck cargo.

Dusty, for it was he, crouched down behind a bollard and tried to think calmly. It was not easy, for his mind was like a firework display with a set piece of whirling catherine wheels and the sudden hissing up-rush of many coloured rockets as, one after another, fresh and more sharply dangerous possibilities flared up in his imagination.

Every word the two men had spoken had spelled peril for his Uncle Hank. What was more, the subject of their talk—stolen jewels—police—pursuit—had a dreadfully familiar ring. His thoughts flew back to his last night in Hull, to the home, if you could call it a home, from which he had fled.

Smiler Huggins and his wife Annie ran a second-hand clothes shop in a squalid alley not far from the docks. It was a dingy little place, reeking of the odours of the discarded garments which hung in drab rows from the ceiling, and spilled untidily from the huge hampers piled against the walls. Just how unsavoury it really was, Dusty was unable to appreciate; he had lived in it so long. In fact, it was the only home he could truly remember, though sometimes, when he was lonely and unhappy, there came to him a dim recollection of another kind of home, and a softly pretty, quiet-spoken woman whom he liked to think of as his real mother. But it was all very vague and far away.

At first, when he was sent to her as a small boy of five, Mrs. Huggins—he had stubbornly refused to call her mother—had made a great fuss of him. He had tried to respond politely, as his mother had taught him, but somehow he could not really be fond of this brassy, over-bearing woman who seemed to want to smother him with her embraces.

A Stowaway and Stolen Jewels

Gradually, as she realized this, a change came over Mrs. Huggins, and lately her conduct had begun to frighten him in a way he could not understand. Often she was out when he came home from school. When she returned, hours later, she seemed unsteady on her feet, and he could not make out what she was saying. At other times, without warning, she would give way to unreasoning fits of rage. Mostly he was able to dodge the sudden blows she aimed at him, but in the gloom of the junk-filled living-room at the back of the shop, no matter how closely he watched, he could not always read the expression in the dark, closely set eyes, nor anticipate the direction of attack.

But that last night had been different. All the evening, while he struggled to fix his attention on his books, he had been aware of her watching and listening. At every clang of the shop bell she had started to her feet and peered through the glass-topped door into the shop, muttering to herself. And when it finally came, the step and the voice she was fearing, it was on him that she had turned.

Involuntarily, his fingers sought the tender bump on the side of his head, and he seemed to hear again the crash of the living-room door as she flung him out into the dark passage. Then, as he had lain sprawling at the foot of the unlighted staircase, he had heard the unhurried entry of the police sergeant, his measured questions and the loud, blustering replies of Smiler, who had followed him in. It was jewels the police were after. That much Dusty had heard before the door to the passage was slammed, and he picked himself up and climbed slowly to his cheerless room.

And now it was jewels again.

What did it all mean?

The Bellamy Jewels

Could it be—and as the thought framed itself in his mind Dusty went pale with horror—could it be that there was some connexion? Had the police been searching the Huggins's premises because of Uncle Hank and the jewels these men said were in his kitbag?

Trembling, Dusty thrust from him the very idea. It was unthinkable that Uncle Hank should have anything to do with stolen jewels. Besides, it was many weeks since he had even been near the shop. Dusty had found out for himself that the *Tilbury Pride* was in dock.

And yet—the men had said it.

Dusty shuddered. It was frightening. Suppose the police found something in Uncle Hank's kitbag?

Through the fog he saw the bosun and a couple of hands going aft. The bosun was carrying a light. Dusty realized that the police must be getting near. Torn with anxiety, he made himself as small as he could and crept a little farther aft. A low gleam of light from a ventilator suggested that he might be able to see down into the fo'c'sle. Snaking his way along, he applied his eyes to the crack.

Down in the fo'c'sle Hank Miller was stowing his kitbag under his bunk, on top of which lay the package of jewels. Hank's brain was a whirl of horrible conjectures, but as yet he had hit on no plan by which to extricate himself and Squeaky from their dilemma, and Squeaky, as Hank had just informed him, was about as much use as a sick 'eadache. Hank turned quickly as Tub and Walrus entered.

"What have you done with that package I gave you to bring aboard at Hull?" said Tub, wasting no time.

"It's 'ere," said Hank shortly, picking up the box, "and you're takin' it over right now."

Tub eyed him acutely.

A Stowaway and Stolen Jewels

" Been having a look-see, eh?"

Hank made no reply. There was a brief silence. Squeaky's eyes were round with fright. Ginger Green, who had withdrawn into the farthest corner of his bunk, was almost beside himself with triumph. He had suffered many a slight from Tub Timkins, and now Tub was going to pay—and pay again. Ginger's palms began to itch in anticipation of the riches to come. But he must wait his chance. Tub was his man. The others were merely small fry.

" Okay. I get it," sneered Tub. " Just a couple of rats. Think you can do a job like this and then back out as soon as you hear a police whistle."

" If I'd 'ave known what was in this box, we'd never 'ave touched it," said Hank angrily, " and you know it, you dirty twister. For two pins I'd knock your block off."

Walrus put up his fists menacingly, but Tub shot him a warning glance. He'd had a flash of inspiration.

" Listen, Miller," he said brutally, " if these jewels are found in this ship there's half a dozen of us can swear that you brought them aboard and that you've had 'em all along. You're going to get up top quick and put 'em in that pump case in the deck cargo."

" Do your own dirty work, Tub Timkins," retorted Hank, still holding out the box. " I won't have nothing more to do with it."

" Nor me neither," piped up Squeaky.

" Shut up!" barked Tub. " You're in this too, up to your neck, and don't forget it. There's just one chance for the two of you. Get the stuff out of the way till the cops have gone."

" Wot, me play 'ide and seek with a gang of coppers and a box of diamonds in me 'and? Not likely!"

The Bellamy Jewels

"Don't be a fool, Miller. The police won't be here yet. They can't board us in five minutes in this weather."

Hank stood irresolute, the box of jewels still in his hand. There was no getting away from it. Tub had the better of them. He made one last effort. "I've a good mind to tell 'em," he began truculently.

"Suit yourself," said Tub sarcastically. "Seven years in clink is a long time to think it over."

"All right," said Hank, with sudden decision. "You've got us proper this time. I'll stick 'em in the pump case where you said, and then I'm through with you and your perishin' jewels."

"At last you're showing some sense," said Tub approvingly. "Now then, that box'll stick out a mile. Better roll 'em in something soft."

He glanced quickly round the quarters, then made a dive at Squeaky. Taken off his guard, Squeaky found his red-spotted muffler whipped from his neck and spread out on a bunk before he could even get his hands to his throat. Horrified and fascinated, he watched while Tub poured into it a sparkling cascade of brooches, rings and necklaces.

"'Ere, that muffler's got my name on it!" he moaned.

"So much the worse for you if it's found," returned Tub, swiftly knotting together the four corners and handing the bundle to Hank. "Now, get along. Be quick and be careful. You'd better go too, Squeaky Watts, and keep a look-out."

For a few seconds Tub stood looking after them. Then, drawing Walrus with him to a bulkhead light, he opened his right hand and disclosed a small glittering object.

"Remember Rita the barmaid at the Dog and Angry Rabbit?" he said, with a broad wink.

"Sure do," grinned Walrus. Rita was a blonde after

his own heart. She reminded him of the Nordic beauties
of his own land.

"Next time we put in to Hull I'm getting engaged to
her," boasted Tub, "and this is the ring that's going to
seal the bargain."

"And wot makes you think she'll 'ave you?" inquired
a coarse, jeering voice from the background.

Tub swung round like a flash, his hand going instantly
to his trousers pocket and his eyes narrowing dangerousy.

"Oh, it's you, is it?" he snarled, surveying Ginger's
rumpled figure and pasty face with a curl of his thin lips.
"And what are you doing down here, may I ask? Sleeping your head off as usual, I suppose?"

Ginger ignored this obvious feeler for information.

"I got as much right 'ere as you," he returned coolly.

"There's some as might think otherwise," said Tub
significantly, glancing at his wrist-watch. "The bosun,
f'rinstance."

"Ah yes—the bosun," said Ginger, lounging forward
insolently. "Now, if I was to tell the bosun, and the
bosun was to tell the——"

"Okay," Tub broke in, abandoning all pretence. "So
you skulked in a bunk and 'eard all about it, did you?"

"Oh, I 'eard this and that," said Ginger airily. "But
wot's a little smugglin' between friends?" he grinned.
"We share and share alike, don't we?"

Tub thought quickly. Time was getting short. He
knew Ginger for a loose-tongued fool. A drink or two
in a dockside tavern and the story would be broadcast.
If he could not be frightened into silence, then he must
be put out of the way till the danger was past.

"And suppose we don't?" he said slowly, closing in.

Ginger was drunk with power. He saw no threat in
Tub's quiet voice and stealthy advance.

The Bellamy Jewels

" Then you and Walrus and Miller and Watts can share it between you," he allowed magnanimously. And he added with a triumphant leer, " In prison."

" In a pig's ear," muttered Tub with cold fury. His right fist shot out and met Ginger's jaw with an ominous thud. Ginger staggered backwards, his feet slid from under him, and the back of his head crashed against the corner of the iron stove. His body slumped to the deck and he lay still, his light-lashed eyes staring upwards unseeingly.

.   .   .   .

When Hank and Squeaky arrived on deck with the bundle of jewels, Hank paused and turned to Squeaky.

" I reckon I'd best do this job on me own," he said tersely. " You get aft and show yerself. You give me the jim-jams."

" Righto," said Squeaky instantly, undisguised relief lighting his frightened features.

" And if anybody asks where I am," added Hank pointedly, " you can tell 'em I'm countin' me blessings."

Squeaky made off without further ado, and Hank moved steadily and noiselessly forward through the fog, skirting the pile of deck cargo on the starboard side of the ship until he came to a large boarded case about as high as a piano and twice as thick, with a peculiar hump at one end. It contained a delivery pump and it was labelled Bickton Gasworks.

Now that there was a hope of getting rid of the jewels, Hank set to work coolly and deliberately. Placing the bundle on the deck at his feet, he took a knife from his pocket, prised away a strip of metal binding, and sprung back a board. The bundle fitted in snugly. Hank pressed the board back into place, restored the metal binding,

A Stowaway and Stolen Jewels

and was about to make his way thankfully aft when he
saw three dim figures rising up from the fo'c'sle companion. As they gained the deck, a vagrant breeze cleared
the mist around them and Hank recognized the taller
figures as those of Tub and Walrus. Between them they
were supporting a third figure.

Hank drew back. Through no fault of his own he
had become involved in a crime for which the penalties
were very heavy. Under ruthless pressure, and to free
himself and Squeaky, he had made himself, in a small
measure, a party to this crime, but he was resolved to
have no further hand in it. By the look of them, Tub
and Walrus were up to no good.

Hank waited, motionless, in the shadows as the three
advanced. They were heading for the port rails. In a
brief gleam of light from a mast-head lantern, he saw
that the third figure was that of Ginger Green. Ginger
appeared to be either sick or intoxicated. His red head
lolled helplessly backwards on his shoulders, his face was
deathly pale, and his mouth hung open.

Curiosity and a mounting apprehension held Hank
rooted to the spot. He watched his two enemies lay the
inert body on the deck.

"Suppose de body's picked up vid de head cracked
in," he heard Walrus say doubtfully. "Von't somebody vant to know who killed him?"

Tub emptied Ginger's trousers pockets with a practised
hand and began stowing the contents in the jacket.

"How will anybody know it's Ginger Green with
nothing in his pockets to say so?" he muttered fiercely,
drawing Ginger's arms out of his jacket. "As for his
head, they'll think he's been hit by a ship's screw. Anyway, he asked for it, interfering little swine! If I'd given
way, he'd have had us in the jug before you could say

knife. He'd never have kept his mouth shut, no matter what I promised him."

Walrus said no more. Tub stood up with the jacket in his hand and produced something from his own pocket. Hank could not see what it was, but, straining his ears, he heard Tub say: " I'm going to put this ring in the pocket of his jacket and then I'm going to make sure that somebody finds it."

" What a brain you got, Tub," said Walrus admiringly.

" D'you know what for?"

Walrus shook his head stupidly. " You ain't told me yet," he said, faintly reproachful.

" What's the use of talking to a dummy like you?" said Tub disgustedly. He bent down. " Catch hold of his feet."

Hank had heard more than enough. Tub's purpose was all too clear. As he sped with horrified haste down the starboard deck, a distant splash came to his ears.

. . . .

Dusty Bates, crouched down beside the fo'c'sle ventilator, waited in a fever of fear and impatience. Without being able to hear what was said, he had nevertheless gathered enough to convince him more than ever of his uncle's danger. When Hank and Squeaky left with the bundle of jewels, he had turned from the ventilator and watched, with his heart in his mouth, while Hank crept forward and completed his dangerous task. Now he could wait no longer. As Hank, fleeing from the dark deeds of Tub and Walrus, came abreast of him, he stood up and put out a cautious hand. " Uncle Hank!" he called softly.

Hank stopped short and peered through the fog. The dire events of this night had crowded so fast upon him that he began to fear he was the victim of delusions.

" God bless my soul!" he ejaculated at last. " Wot are
you doin' 'ere, Dusty?"

But even as he spoke, his mind began to clear. This
was no delusion. The boy was there before him, drat
him, and, angry though he was, Hank's protective instincts
lent speed to his usually slow thoughts. How long had
the boy been there? Had he seen the ruthless deed that
he himself had just witnessed? Quickly he stooped down
to Dusty's eye level and forced his gaze back to the spot
by the port rails. With a grunt of relief he straightened
himself.

" Why did you do that, Uncle Hank?" said Dusty, who
had been watching him curiously.

Hank thought carefully before he replied. He had
assured himself that the boy could have seen nothing
from where he now stood. But suppose he had been
elsewhere?

" A sailor 'as to keep 'is eyes skinned all the time,
Dusty," he said artfully. " I was just tryin' to see wot you
was lookin' at from 'ere."

" I was only waiting for you to come along," Dusty
told him. " I wasn't looking at anything."

" So you didn't see nothink?" pursued Hank, watching
him closely.

" No," replied Dusty uncertainly, for it was by no
means the truth. " What was there to see?"

" Nothink," said Hank shortly.

Dusty thought this an odd conversation, but he did
not linger over it for there were other and more important
things on his mind. He wanted to warn Hank about
what he had heard those men say, but somehow it was
difficult to start. Now that he was face to face with his
uncle, it seemed like treachery even to think of it.

As for Hank, relieved though he was that the boy

hadn't seen what happened at the rail, there still remained his unexpected and embarrassing presence to be accounted for.

"Now then," he said harshly, his anger rising as his immediate anxiety died down, "p'raps you'll be good enough to explain yourself?"

Dusty hung his head. All his pent-up affection and loyalty were centred on Hank. He could not bear his displeasure.

"You promised you'd stay at 'ome and be a good boy, after last time," Hank continued angrily. The boy was his only nephew and he was very fond of him, but Hank had a jewel robbery and a murder on his mind, and further to adjust himself to the appearance of a stowaway relative was taxing his powers to the limit.

"I know, Uncle Hank," Dusty admitted desperately, "but you don't know what it's like. It's a beastly place. It stinks. And so does Mrs. Huggins," he added defiantly, the recollection of her gin-laden breath almost causing him to retch.

Hank paused, arrested by the boy's voice and expression. Once or twice lately, on his periodic visits, he had seen and heard things which had caused him some uneasiness, and from time to time his conscience had been inconveniently active.

"They don't want me there," cried Dusty. "There's things going on that they don't want me to know about. *Please*, Uncle Hank," he begged, clasping Hank's arm in urgent appeal, "let me stay with you!"

"But wot am I goin' to do with you, Dusty?" demanded Hank, almost at his wit's end. "I can't look after you. I've got enough to worry about as it is."

"I *know*," said Dusty earnestly. "That's what I wanted to tell you. That man Tub. I heard him say——"

A Stowaway and Stolen Jewels

" Wot's that?" exclaimed Hank, startled. " Tell me quick, Dusty. Wot did you 'ear?"

" Well, when I was hiding I heard a man called Tub talking to a foreign-sounding man. He said he was going to make you take the stuff ashore, and if anything happened you'd be for it."

" That's right," confirmed a low voice behind them.

The man and boy swung round.

" Quite a clever little snooper, your nephew, Miller," continued Tub, his sharp eyes probing like gimlets. " And what else do you know, young man?"

" You lay orf of 'im, Tub Timkins. He don't know nothin'. Do you, Dusty?"

" N-no, Uncle," stammered Dusty, shrinking away.

Tub bore down upon him, thrusting Hank aside. The police boat was coming alongside. He could hear the bosun's voice shouting directions to its crew. The hunt was on.

" Get this, you miserable little rat," he said, spitting the words out with venomous intensity, " you've *seen* nothing. You've *heard* nothing. Understand?" He gripped the boy's shoulder with fingers of steel; his voice sank to a blood-chilling undertone. " One word from you, and I'll tear the living guts out of you."

He flung the boy away and, with a last malevolent glare at Hank, disappeared into the enveloping fog.

Hank gazed after him with smouldering eyes, his mind a turmoil of rage at his own helplessness and fear for the boy beside him. Then, putting a protective arm round Dusty's trembling figure, he drew him down to the comforting warmth and shelter of the fo'c'sle.

. . . .

When a ship is nearing port, the captain is a very busy man. And so it was with concealed impatience that Captain

The Bellamy Jewels

Ford received in his chart-room Detective-Inspector White and his colleague Johnson. It was, he supposed, merely a routine inspection, or maybe a River Police exercise. All the same, it was as well to be civil. He had already ordered coffee to be served and was prepared to give up a short time to amiable conversation. He was therefore surprised when Detective-Inspector White, the senior of his two visitors, announced that they were hoping to get on to the trail of some stolen jewels.

" But why pick on my ship?" he inquired jocularly.

Inspector White, a distinguished-looking middle-aged man in plain clothes, smiled with tired wisdom.

" Because your vessel sailed from Hull," he explained quietly. " They traced the jewels that far and then lost the scent completely. It is thought that the robbery is the work of an international gang using ordinary seamen to smuggle the stuff aboard small coastal ships and thus get it across to the Continent."

" I see," said Captain Ford, more seriously.

The door opened and a steward entered with a tray of steaming coffee in large white cups.

" Put it down here, Steward," said the captain, indicating the desk before him, " and ask the bosun to come here at once."

" Aye, aye, sir."

The steward withdrew, and Captain Ford passed each man a drink.

" Has this robbery been reported in the papers?" he inquired. " There's been nothing on the radio."

" No. The story hasn't been released yet. As a matter of fact, between ourselves, it's a particularly nasty affair. The jewels had been given for sale by a wealthy and generous woman, a Mrs. Bellamy. The proceeds were to endow a home for sick and needy children from dockyard areas."

A Stowaway and Stolen Jewels

Captain Ford shook his head gravely.

" Well, if there's anything odd going on in the fo'c'sle of this ship, the bosun will have a very good idea. Ah, here he is, I think."

There entered a wiry, energetic-looking little man, smart and alert in appearance. Over his arm he carried a seaman's jacket.

" Detective-Inspector White. Mr. Sullivan. Mr. White has a few questions to ask you about the crew, Sullivan. He's investigating——"

" Excuse me, sir," the bosun broke in volubly, " I must first tell you that one of the men, Ginger Green, has left the ship."

Captain Ford frowned. The two detectives exchanged glances.

" Left the ship?"

" Jumped overboard, sir. One of the hands saw him go. He must have heard the police were coming aboard."

" Do you know anything about this man?"

" Not much, sir, except that he was a lazy, shifty sort of beggar, always dodging the column. Somebody picked up his jacket. I brought it along."

Captain Ford took the garment and passed it to the inspector, who began at once to go through the pockets.

" Here's his paybook and a couple of letters." He glanced at them quickly. ". . . from a girl in Hull . . . a racing paper . . . cigarettes . . . and—what's this? A diamond ring! H'm, a valuable one. I wouldn't be surprised if this is part of the Bellamy lot, Captain. Maybe we're on to something after all."

" Well," said Captain Ford, astounded, " I must say I didn't expect anything like this. Where did we find this Ginger Green, Sullivan?"

" He joined a couple of trips ago, sir, at Hull."

"I wonder if he took the rest of the stuff with him," mused the inspector.

"Could be," rejoined the captain.

"Well, it looks as though our business lies ashore, but we'll go over the ship now we're here." The inspector turned to his colleague. "Johnson, get a description of the missing man and send the launch back to report to Inspector Hallett. Get word to all stations, and organize a thorough search on board."

Then, to Captain Ford, who had risen and picked up his cap: "Don't let me hold you up, Captain. Thanks for your help. I'll just get a few more particulars from Mr. Sullivan."

"Right," said the captain. "I'll see you before you go. In the meantime, I'll get the crew rounded up for Johnson."

Outside, the atmosphere had cleared slightly. The ship was throbbing steadily but slowly up-stream. Shore lights were now visible here and there, and the noise of fog signals was becoming less insistent. The pilot and the mate stood chatting together on the bridge with the helmsman on duty behind them. Captain Ford joined them.

"Muster the crew by the galley, Mister Mate," he ordered, "and give the police any help they may need."

"Aye, aye, sir."

The mate disappeared down the companion-way to the deck and Captain Ford stood gazing moodily ahead. This development he felt to be something of a slur on his ship, though heaven knew it was hard enough to get a full ship's company together these days, and downright impossible to inquire into the past history of every man taken on.

"I think the fog's lifting, Captain," remarked the pilot, after a few minutes' silence.

A Stowaway and Stolen Jewels

" Yes," agreed Ford absently. " I must leave you again for a bit. I want to have a look round."

On the deck below stood Hank Miller, trying to screw up his courage to approach the captain. Hank had been doing some pretty steady thinking. He had not been a sailor for forty years without learning when to turn a blind eye, but murder was a stark horror which could not be ignored. Had it not been for Dusty, he thought, he would have made a clean breast of the whole business. Now his one concern was to protect the boy.

Hank was not much given to reading newspapers, but in his mind's eye he could see a screaming headline " STOWAWAY BOY QUESTIONED IN " TILBURY PRIDE " KILLING!" and he shuddered to think of his dead sister's son exposed to the merciless publicity of a murder trial. No. Even though it meant shielding Tub and Walrus, Hank would keep his dread knowledge to himself. He thanked heaven that Squeaky had not seen what he had seen. So far, there was no suggestion of murder. There was a story going round the ship that Ginger had jumped overboard. It was no surprise to Hank to hear that his coat had been found and was in the possession of the police.

But that was not all. There were worse dangers close at hand. Tub and Walrus were desperate men. Already, Hank knew, Tub suspected that the boy had knowledge which might lead to their undoing. Dusty must be placed beyond their reach without delay, and the only way Hank knew of accomplishing this was to hand him over to the captain.

As the captain descended, Hank braced himself and stepped forward.

" Excuse me, sir."

" What is it, Miller?" the captain replied curtly.

Hank hesitated. Now that it had come to the point, it was more difficult that he had imagined.

"It's—it's a stowaway, sir."

The captain made an exasperated gesture.

"Good heavens! Robberies, men overboard, stowaways. What next?"

"It's my nephew, sir," Hank struggled on. "I've—I've just found him."

The captain's manner softened slightly. Miller was an old hand, a decent steady chap.

"How old is he?"

"About twelve, sir. He's an orphan," explained Hank, seizing his advantage, "and a good lad really, but 'e's been put to live with some folk as don't treat 'im right. And 'e's mad to be a sailor, like me," he added, a trifle sheepishly.

"H'm," said the captain, suppressing a smile. "You know, of course, that it is a serious offence to stow away, even for a boy," he added severely.

"Yes, sir," admitted Hank meekly.

"I'll have to see him and hand him over to the police welfare people. Has he had any food?"

"Squeaky—I mean Watts—is giving him some now, sir."

"Well, I can't do anything about it to-night, I'm too busy. Keep an eye on him and I'll see him in the morning."

"Thank you, sir."

CHAPTER II

Dusty gives a Promise

When Dusty awoke next morning he was puzzled, at first, to know where he was. He raised himself on one elbow and looked round. Opposite him were three bunks, one above the other, all empty and disordered. He himself was in a bottom bunk and he supposed there were two more above him, but there was no sign that they were occupied. On the floor beside him there was a mug of milk and a plate of biscuits. Dusty took a long drink and began to munch contentedly.

Good old Uncle Hank, he thought. He'd not been nearly so angry as Dusty had feared. Perhaps, after all, he wouldn't be handed over to the police. The police! Dusty sat up abruptly. Last night, what with being so tired and frightened and not wanting to upset Uncle Hank again, he'd said no more about the jewels and his knowledge of their hiding-place. Fully alert now, he realized that the engines had stopped and that there were loud thumping noises overheard. He could hear the rattle of machinery and the voices of men shouting. They must be unloading the cargo. At any moment the case containing the jewels might be moved. He must find out what was happening. He threw back the blankets, slipped on his jacket and trousers and shoes, smoothed down his rumpled dark hair, and ran up on deck.

The fog had vanished magically. The river sparkled in the morning sunshine. Dusty lifted his head and took a deep breath. Excitedly he looked around him. There was the mountain of deck cargo, still untouched. Nobody was about. He passed round the corner of the deck-house and walked along to the after part of the ship.

The hatch covering had been removed and, operating from the dock-side, a vast overhead travelling crane was steadily transferring the contents of the hold. In charge of a gang of men was the bosun, his cap on the back of his head and his fist full of papers.

Dusty edged nearer, fascinated by the movements of the crane. What fun to be in charge of such a monster, he thought. He shaded his eyes with his hand. From the window of the control cabin a man in oily overalls and a peaked cap was looking down at the ship, watching for the bosun's signals, his arms moving as he worked the controls.

Dusty felt a touch on his shoulder and turned to find the burly figure of Hank beside him.

" Isn't it wonderful, Uncle Hank ?"

" Yes, boy," agreed Hank. But he spoke absently, and Dusty could see that his attention was elsewhere. Following his uncle's gaze, he saw two men in civilian clothes pass down the after gangway from ship to dock-side. One of them was a tall, grey-haired man wearing a black trilby hat. Dusty thought he looked like a doctor.

" Them's detectives," said Hank in respectful tones.

Dusty nodded, somewhat awed by this information.

" And you can thank your lucky stars Captain Ford didn't hand you over, my lad."

" What's he going to do with me, Uncle Hank? Couldn't I be a cabin boy, or something?"

" Cabin boy ?" Hank smiled. " Wot d'you think this is—the *Queen Mary* ?" He was silent for a moment before he added: " It's a good job Alice ain't 'ere. Nice thing if she was to 'ear you talk about bein' a cabin boy."

Dusty gives a Promise

"Alice?" said Dusty wonderingly. "Who's Alice?"

"Alice was my young sister and your mother," came the unexpected reply.

Dusty's eyes glowed, but he kept a firm hold on himself. Many a time in the past he'd asked Uncle Hank to tell him about his mother, for he knew they'd been brother and sister, but Hank had always brushed the topic aside and brought up something else. He'd tried Mrs. Huggins too, but he soon found out that the subject annoyed her. So now he choked back the eager questions which came flying to his lips, and asked as casually as he could: "What did my mother want me to be, then?"

"She wanted you to be an officer, Dusty boy; right from the time you was born, she did."

"Me an officer?" said Dusty, with a surprised grin. "But officers are important people; I mean, not people like us."

Hank snorted. "You needn't go judging yer mother by me," he retorted tartly. "I'm one thing: she was another. Yer mother was quite an eddicated woman, my boy."

This was a new idea to Dusty, and not at all an unpleasant one. He let his thoughts play round it for a moment, but it wouldn't do to let Uncle Hank lose interest. An opportunity like this might never come again.

"Then why weren't you educated too, Uncle Hank?" he pursued.

"Because I'm a fool, that's why," replied Hank bitterly. "If I'd 'ave known then wot I know now, I'd 'ave been different to wot I was then and different to wot I am now."

For the time being this complex statement put an end to Dusty's questions. While he was struggling to unravel it Hank, still following his wounding ruminations, went on: "I was a fool, that's wot I was. For wot it's worth," he said, with faint derision, "I might 'ave been an *eddi-cated* fool. But I couldn't stick it, and that's why I run away to sea. It was a rough life and I got rough to suit. And that's wot I don't want you to be."

This was a long speech for Hank, and by the end of it Dusty was touched almost to tears.

"But, Uncle Hank," he protested, "I'd rather be like you than anyone I've ever seen."

Hank patted the boy's head and smiled. "That's because you ain't seen much, Dusty boy," he said. He put his arm round Dusty's shoulders and stared thoughtfully over the ship's side into the river. "I could 'ave sworn them 'Uggins would bring you up proper when they was so keen on 'avin' you," he remarked.

"D'you know what I think, Uncle Hank?" said Dusty, struggling free. "I think Mrs. Huggins hated me because she hasn't got any children of her own," he declared hotly. "If ever I asked her about my own mother, she'd make me scrub the floor or something, and then hit me because I wasn't doing it fast enough. And there are other things," he went on darkly, "things I've never told you."

"Then p'raps you'd better not," Hank said quickly, "because when I get back to 'Ull there might be trouble." He sighed wearily. "And I've got all the trouble I want."

"I'm sorry, Uncle Hank," said Dusty, seeing the troubles furrowing Hank's weather-beaten countenance.

"It serves me right, boy," said Hank resignedly. "I've always done the right thing at the wrong time, as the sayin' is. Look at the mess I'm in now!"

"Yes, I know," said Dusty, but he was determined not to be side-tracked; he must gain all the knowledge he could while Hank was in a communicative mood. "Uncle Hank," he said, "why don't you ever talk about my father? What did *he* want me to be?"

Hank's clean-shaven lips folded themselves together in an obstinate line and he looked somehow uncomfortable. Dusty felt a sharp twinge of disappointment, for it seemed as though Uncle Hank was going to dry up.

"We fell out at the weddin'," he said at last. "'E didn't like the way I was dressed, for a start. After I'd got a special rig-out too," he added indignantly.

It was clear that Uncle Hank had a grievance and that, whatever it was exactly, it still rankled. But to Dusty, so nearly within grasp of a real background for himself, it seemed of small account.

"Did my father want me to be an officer too?" he persisted.

"'E didn't want you to be nothink," Hank returned gruffly, "because 'e was drownded at sea soon after you was born."

"Was he a sailor too?" asked Dusty avidly.

"'E was a nothink," Hank said tersely, his mind still on that past grievance.

"But you said he was drowned at sea," Dusty reminded him.

Hank made an impatient gesture. "'E was a stooard, that's wot 'e was, if you *must* know," he said. "Stooard!" He spat the word out contemptuously. "Talkin' to me!"

Dusty could see that this was a very sore point, but he was ignorant, as yet, of the hierarchy of life at sea, and the depth of Hank's feelings puzzled him.

"Isn't it nice to be a steward, Uncle Hank?"

"Nice!" echoed Hank, staring. "Nice to be a stooard? Listen, Dusty boy. If ever you get to sea, regular like, you'll find out that there's two sorts aboard ships. One's officers and the other's seamen." He paused and spat accurately over the side. " Stooards don't count." And with one wave of a work-calloused hand and the corners of his mouth turned down, Hank dismissed the entire race of ships' stewards. " Not but wot your father 'adn't seen better times," he amended, relenting slightly at sight of Dusty's downcast expression, " but that's wot 'e was at the finish."

Dusty's face brightened as his mind fastened on the romantic possibilities contained in this last observation, but, before he could frame any further questions, Hank brought him back to the complicated present with a jerk.

" Wot's more important than all that," he pointed out with sudden briskness, " is wot they're goin' to do about you."

" Oh, Uncle Hank," pleaded Dusty, " please don't let them send me back."

" It ain't in my 'ands, boy," said Hank kindly. " I told the captain why you run away, and 'e said 'e'd think it over. 'E's got kids of 'is own and maybe 'e'll find some way out for you. I expect 'e'll send for you presently, so don't go away."

" No, Uncle," but he spoke mechanically, because he had just remembered what had brought him up on deck in the first place.

" I say, Uncle Hank, they didn't find those brooches and things, did they?"

Hank gripped the boy's arm.

" 'Ere, wot's that you're sayin'?" he said in a startled voice.

" The rings and things in that bundle," said Dusty nervously.

Hank took a quick look round and drew the boy out of earshot. Still holding him fast, he said hoarsely:

Dusty gives a Promise

"Now then, boy, let's get to the bottom o' this. Wot did you see?"

Dusty wriggled himself free.

"I—I only saw the jewellery you put in that case," he faltered.

"Wot else?" demanded Hank sharply.

"I saw Tub Timkins talking to you down in the fo'c'sle, but I couldn't hear what he was saying. Are *you* afraid of him too, Uncle Hank?"

Hank evaded the question. "He's a bad man, Dusty," he asserted.

"And what about those jewels?" A thrilling idea occurred to Dusty. "Is it *smuggling*, Uncle Hank?"

For a moment Hank was at a loss for an answer. Smuggling it was, and a good deal more besides, but thank God the boy had seen nothing of the brutal killing of Ginger Green.

"Not exactly, Dusty," he said, after a pause. "Squeaky and me, we're just sort o' mindin' 'em."

"Oh," said Dusty, disappointed. "I thought perhaps it was a nice big adventure, like I've read about."

Hank permitted himself a twisted smile. "It's an adventure all right," he said wryly, "but it ain't a nice one."

"What's going to happen to the jewels?"

Hank did not reply at once, for this was a problem which continually nagged at his honest mind.

"I don't know yet, Dusty," he said at last, "but I want you to understand this: I been a bit of a mug, see? But I never done wrong on purpose."

"Oh no, Uncle Hank," replied Dusty fervently. "I know that. I wish I could do something to help."

"So you can, boy. All you got to do is keep yer mouth shut. One word to Captain Ford or anybody, and I'll be in gaol."

"I won't tell a soul," said Dusty solemnly. "I promise."

"That's a good boy," said Hank, patting his shoulder. "Now I must get back to work or the bosun'll be after me. You stick around till the captain sends for you."

"Uncle Hank," said Dusty hesitatingly, as Hank turned to go, "is——"

"Don't you worry, Dusty," said Hank, sensing the boy's unspoken fear. "I got me eye on Tub Timkins."

.　.　.　.　.　.　.　.　.

Not very far away, the question of the fate of the Bellamy jewels was exercising other minds.

In a small room on the fourth floor of a block of dockside offices, a dark, polished-looking gentleman, smartly dressed, and wearing horn-rimmed spectacles, looked gravely across his orderly desk at an unexpected caller.

The interview had been in progress only a short time, but it was the urgent desire of the dark gentleman that it should end with all speed, for the visitor had brought news by no means to his liking. Moreover, from the adjoining room there came sounds of explosive argument on the telephone, and it seemed likely that at any moment he might be interrupted with most unfortunate results.

If the visitor considered these sounds in any way unusual, or was even aware of them, he gave no sign. Picking up his black trilby hat from the desk, he rose to his feet. The dark gentleman also rose.

"As you are the London manager," concluded Inspector White, "I thought it right to let you know immediately, Mr. Merryvale."

"Indeed, yes," agreed the other suavely. "I can't tell you how much I appreciate your promptness," he went on, neatly edging his visitor towards the door. "It is most disturbing to learn that a member of one of our crews is mixed up in such a shocking robbery. I shall report the matter to my head office at once." He held out his hand. " Good day, Inspector. I wish you all luck in tracing the missing man."

" Thank you," said the inspector, shaking the proffered hand. " I'll keep in touch with you," he added, with a level glance.

" Do," urged the dark gentleman smoothly.

He had scarcely closed the door, which bore a sign reading " Ixion Steamship Co. London Manager—J. Merryvale ", before an inner door was thrust open and there entered swiftly a short, sandy-haired young man in a shabby suit, with a battered felt hat on the back of his head and a damp cigarette hanging from the corner of his mouth. His evident intention of bursting into speech was silenced by an imperious gesture from Merryvale.

" Haven't you got more sense than to bawl your head off on the telephone when I've got a visitor?" he demanded, whipping off his glasses angrily. " Who was it?"

" Captain Fernandez," replied the other sullenly. " Says he's sailing for Amsterdam on this tide with or without the Bellamy lot."

" Well, why isn't the stuff here?" snapped Merryvale. " What's happened to Timkins?"

Joe Stark shrugged his thin shoulders insolently and shifted his cigarette to the other side of his mouth.

" Dodged ashore," he replied briefly, " as soon as I got on board."

" But surely you had a word with him?" said Merryvale, his eyes glinting dangerously.

" How could I, with a couple of wide-eyed flatfoots nosey-parkering around? Besides, Timkins kept out of my way deliberately."

" H'm," said Merryvale, beginning to pace angrily back

and forth. "There's some dirty work going on somewhere. And, what is more, Scotland Yard is on to it. That fellow I had in here just now was Detective-Inspector White. Came to inform me that he'd found a ring from the Bellamy collection in the pocket of a jacket left behind by a fellow who'd jumped overboard. Ginger Green. Never heard of him. Have you?"

Stark shook his head.

"Well, there's no time to waste if we're to get the stuff away. See if you can get Timkins at the hostel."

Stark picked up the telephone receiver and dialled a number.

.   .   .   .

In the dayroom of the crew hostel of the Ixion Steamship Company four men were seated on forms at a long table scattered with dirty crockery and stained with the aftermath of countless meals.

It was a gloomy apartment, its walls adorned only with a notice-board and an old-fashioned telephone fixture, and its murky whitewashed windows giving straight on to the brick wall of a basement area topped by rusty iron railings. Inside, facing the windows, a door opened on to a passage leading to a primitive washroom and sleeping-quarters. In the far corner of the room there was a sink with running water, and a gas ring, kettle, and frying-pan stood on a small table beside it.

Despite the evidence of a recent meal, the atmosphere between the four men was far from convivial. Tub Timkins, his arms folded and his chair tilted back, surveyed Hank and Squeaky through a haze of cigarette smoke, his eyes half closed. Beside him, Walrus was working his way steadily through a plateful of assorted food which he had fried for himself.

Hank gazed morosely into his empty cup and went over

Dusty gives a Promise

endlessly in his mind the events of the previous night, vainly trying to find some way of reconciling his duty to the captain with his desire to shield Dusty, for Hank's conscience was beginning to work overtime. On the way to the hostel he had rashly yielded to an impulse to confide in Squeaky the truth about Ginger Green's disappearance, and although the sharing of this grisly secret had afforded him temporary relief, Squeaky's reception of the news, as he might have expected, was the reverse of comforting. Squeaky was aghast.

When the strident peal of the telephone bell cut through the strained silence of the dayroom, Squeaky was in the act of raising his third cup of tea to his lips. He started violently and dropped the cup with a crash.

Hank glared. He might have known Squeaky would lose his nerve. He made a move to rise.

" Stay where you are," ordered Tub peremptorily. " If it ain't Merryvale himself, it'll be that Stark. Let 'em ring, the rattlesnakes."

" Ho-ho!" rumbled Walrus, his mouth full of bread and sausage. " Rattlesnakes! Dat's good, Tub."

The bell rang on, insistent, impersonal. Squeaky shifted his bony shanks nervously on the hard form.

" It might be somebody else," he suggested shakily, his discomfort increasing as Tub fixed him with a malevolent eye.

" Such as who?" inquired Tub.

" I'm thinking about Ginger Green," quavered Squeaky.

At the mention of this name Hank shook himself and then, as though he had at last received a signal he had been waiting for, his features became set in stubborn purpose.

" So am I," he announced resolutely, " and it's wot I am goin' to 'ave settled." His voice strengthened as the full sense of his wrongs gathered in his mind. " I been a mug, as usual," he accused himself, glowering at Tub. "Wot I shoulda done when I spotted them jewels was to go straight to the captain. But you stopped me with your slimy talk." He half rose from his seat in sudden determination. "I'm goin' to make a clean breast of it now—all of it—and chance wot 'appens."

Tub's reaction to this threat was more than strange; it was startling. The look on his face became innocently puzzled, and when he spoke his voice was as mild as milk.

"What are you talking about, Miller?" he inquired smoothly.

"You know wot I'm talkin' about," charged Hank loudly. "The murder of Ginger Green, that's wot I'm talkin' about."

Squeaky's mouth was agape. Even Walrus had ceased to stuff himself.

Hank leaned on the table, thrust his face forward, and fairly spluttered with rage.

"Didn't I see you dump 'im overboard after you done 'im in—you and Walrus?" he demanded, almost beside himself.

Tub turned to Walrus, whose expression betokened a profound bewilderment.

"Did you hear that, Walrus?" he inquired, cleverly simulating horrified surprise. "Miller's saying we killed Ginger Green and dumped him over the side. Us," he repeated incredulously, tapping himself and Walrus on the chest. "You and me!"

Walrus fumbled heavily for a correct answer to this but he soon gave it up in favour of his usual refuge. He squared his great right fist and stroked it fondly with his left hand.

"How if I give him a nice loud kiss vid dis, Tub?" he suggested lovingly.

Dusty gives a Promise

Tub brushed the idea aside with a contemptuous gesture and transferred his attention to the gaping Squeaky.

" Did you see what Miller says he saw, Squeaky ?" he asked in a voice of patient inquiry.

Squeaky shook his head vacantly. Events had taken such a curious turn that Squeaky was powerless to keep up with them.

" Hank told me about it," he stammered.

Tub came back to the outraged and mystified Hank. " Did your nephew see it ?"

" No, 'e never," snorted Hank, " and that's the only good thing in the 'ole dirty bag o' tricks. Are there any more silly questions you want to ask before I go and get it off me chest ?"

Tub made a galvanic movement. His manner changed. " Yes, one," he said, and his voice cracked out sharply. " You seem to be mighty certain that Ginger Green was killed and dumped overboard. This is the question I want to ask, Miller." Tub pointed his words with an urgent forefinger directed at Hank like a pistol. " Did *you* kill Ginger Green and dump him over the side with the idea you could blame it on us—me and poor Walrus here ?"

Walrus gave a loud whoop and brought his great fists down on the table so that the crockery danced and rattled. At last he began to divine Tub's purpose.

" Yaas, dat's it, Tub," he gloated. " Vhat a snake to go to sea vid !"

Squeaky was so completely dumbfounded that, for the moment, he ceased even to be frightened. Words failed him except, of course, for his one favourite expression. " Well, I'll go ter me tea !" he gasped.

Hank subsided slowly into his seat and stared, utterly confounded, at the now reproachful-looking Tub. The audacity of the move had taken Hank's breath away; his simple, straightforward mind was incapable of dealing with such a situation. Hank had only the haziest notion of the workings of law and logic. He was convinced that witnesses were of paramount importance in relation to misdeeds, and here he was brought face to face with the fact that there were two against one; two barefaced swindlers and murderers, it is true, but none the less two voices to his one. Nobody else had seen what he had seen.

The telephone began to ring again and the four men waited in silence, each in his own thoughts, until it ceased. Then Tub spoke, softly, but with an undeniable note of complete mastery.

"I think we'd better forget all about Ginger Green, Miller," he remarked temperately. And Hank, baffled and hamstrung, was silent.

In truth, Tub Timkins was well satisfied. He had been expecting some such scene and he was conscious that he had handled it with conspicuous skill. Lighting a fresh cigarette, he turned briskly to another matter.

"The only thing we've got to consider now is how to get our hands on those jewels. And that's another point," he went on, glancing from one to the other. "We, the four of us here—and Miller's nephew," he added, so quietly that it was almost to himself, "are the only people who know the stuff is in that case."

"I ain't touchin' it," Hank muttered under his breath.

"None of us can touch it now till it's in the warehouse, and then you'll do as you're told," Tub informed him brusquely.

"But why should we worry?" piped Squeaky, whose wits were beginning to revive. "Let Mr. Merryvale get it himself."

Dusty gives a Promise

Tub smiled openly. "How can he," he asked, "when he don't know it's there?"

"But you've got to tell 'im," retorted Squeaky boldly. "You're doin' the job for 'im. You said so."

Tub's glance was downright pitying. "We know where it is; Merryvale and his lot don't," he repeated, with such unmistakable emphasis that his meaning sank at once into Squeaky's mind. Squeaky's eyebrows shot up like rockets.

"D'you mean ter say you're goin' to doublecross 'im as well?" he cried shrilly. "Why, we shall 'ave the 'tecs after us on one side and Merryvale and 'is lot after us on the other and——"

"And we shall have what they're all looking for and can't find," purred Tub, "and a whole stack of money to share out. At least," he paused, "me and Walrus will. You two mugs don't deserve a full share."

Squeaky gazed at him with a sort of reluctant admiration. "A crook as big as you ought by rights to be a millionaire in 'is own yacht," he declared, "instead of a 'and aboard a tramp."

"Or 'ung," was Hank's terse alternative.

And then, as if the effort of making a remark had called his subdued faculties into action once more, Hank jumped to his feet.

"I ain't takin' any of your dirty money, 'owever much you get, Tub Timkins!" he cried. "No," he affirmed, with a glance all round, "and nothing won't make me."

Tub rose also and leaned across the table towards him.

"You can please yourself about that, Miller," he retorted, with an unpleasant edge to his low voice, "but you're with us as long as we want you—*and you can't get out*." Again he stressed the point with that forceful forefinger. "That's the thing to remember. Keep it well in your silly head. And one thing more," he added, moving towards the door, " mind that nephew nuisance don't talk too much before I get a chance to tell him why he mustn't."

" Ho-ho!" interpolated Walrus, but instantly shut his mouth on a look from Tub.

" Don't forget, Miller," concluded Tub, as he and Walrus reached the area door, " it's for his sake more than anybody's—now."

Hank said nothing and a few minutes later he and Squeaky also left the hostel together. As they turned the corner a thought occurred to Squeaky.

" 'Ere, Hank," he said, " will them bloodthirsty crooks get up to any 'anky panky with young Dusty?"

" Let 'em try," answered Hank broodingly. " 'E's safe with the captain aboard just now, and before it's dark we'll see if 'e wants any lookin' after." He turned into the open door of a tavern. " Let's go in 'ere for a drink. I want to wash the nasty taste o' them two out of me mouth."

．　．　．　．　．　．　．　．　．

For an hour or more after his uncle had left him, Dusty found plenty of amusement. When he had tired of watching the unloading, he hung over the ship's side gazing about with lively interest. He had never been to London before. Down-stream he recognized Tower Bridge. He had seen many pictures of it. As he watched, the lower span parted and a small steamer bustled between the upraised arms. Dusty's eyes ranged along the grey soot-streaked buildings on the far bank till they were held by the clustering towers and high walls of the Tower of London. That ancient gateway giving on to the water-front had opened to receive many illustrious persons, two of them princes who were boys like himself, never, alas, to be seen alive again.

Presently he became aware of a delicious smell of frying bacon. At the same time he discovered that he was hungry. He left the rail and wandered aft till he came to the open door of the galley.

" 'Ullo, mate," said the cook, a cheerful and garrulous Cockney by name of Bob Pepper. " Wot are you doin' 'ere?"

" I'm waiting to see the captain," replied Dusty.

" Goin' ter sign on for the next trip, eh?"

" I'd like to," admitted Dusty seriously, " but my Uncle Hank says I'm too young."

" I reckon 'e's right, at that," remarked Bob, slapping a sizzling rasher between two thick slices of bread and holding it out. " 'Ere you are. That'll make the 'air grow on yer chest."

" Oh—thank you," grinned Dusty.

" That's okay, son," said his new acquaintance with a generous wink. " I got boys of me own. You better run along now. I'm busy."

Dusty sauntered back to the sunny side of the ship, enjoying the good food. With his back to the river, he leaned against the rail and met the impersonal gaze of a large tabby cat sitting neat and composed at the foot of the steps leading to the bridge. After a few seconds it rose, arched its back, stretched its hind legs luxuriously, and advanced with jungle grace towards him, uttering a polite " Miaouw!"

" Hullo, Pussy," said Dusty, who was fond of cats.

The animal seated itself at his feet and fixed large yellow eyes on the remains of the sandwich. Dusty dropped a few scraps. The cat disposed of them delicately and commenced to rub itself to and fro against his legs.

The Bellamy Jewels

Dusty stooped and gathered the soft warm creature into his arms. He stroked it gently, and was rewarded with a satisfied purring. Without taking much notice, he was aware that somebody was descending from the bridge.

The footsteps ceased suddenly and he looked up to meet the blue eyes of a boy about his own age. They were not particularly friendly eyes; indeed, Dusty saw at once that they were very much the reverse. He saw, too, that the boy was tidily dressed and had well-brushed fair hair, which was not very much in his favour. He stared back with equal hostility.

"What are you doing with that cat?" demanded the newcomer aggressively.

"Stroking it," replied Dusty shortly. "Why?"

The boy descended the rest of the steps.

"It doesn't like being stroked."

"Oh yes, it does. It's purring." Dusty began to feel annoyed. "Who d'you think you are, anyway?"

"My father's captain of this ship."

"Well, he's not captain of this cat," retorted Dusty.

"That's enough of your sauce," said the other hotly, making a grab for the animal. "Put it down."

The cat leapt to the deck and scampered off. Dusty, now thoroughly roused, doubled up his fists and delivered a smart punch on the jaw. This was returned with angry force. The captain's son was the taller by several inches and his reach was longer, but Dusty was tough and well able to take care of himself. Without either boy gaining the advantage, they were both red in the face and breathless when a sturdy little figure pushed itself between them, and a girl's voice cried: "You ought to be ashamed of yourself, David. Where are your manners?"

David brushed his hair from his eyes and glared at Dusty. "He started it!"

Dusty gives a Promise

"I don't care who started it. He's smaller than you."

The girl turned to Dusty with motherly concern.

"Did he hurt you?"

"He couldn't!" snorted Dusty, glaring back at David.

"We'll see about that," muttered David. He lunged forward violently, but the girl, whose name was Shelagh, was too quick for him. Once more she came between them. "Stop it, David!" she cried, stamping her foot.

David stepped back, scowling.

"All right. But you wait," he threatened.

"You'd better go and tidy yourself," Shelagh advised him dispassionately.

"Mind your own business," returned David, and moved sulkily away to lean over the ship's side.

Shelagh turned brightly to Dusty, who was beginning to be somewhat alarmed by this display of feminine management.

"Are you the boy who stowed away?"

"Yes," admitted Dusty, with some reserve.

"I've got to take you to Mummy and Daddy in the chartroom. They want to talk to you."

"What about?" asked Dusty, playing for time. He certainly didn't like David and he wasn't at all sure he enjoyed being championed by this bossy little girl. If they were samples of the Ford family, he probably wouldn't like Mummy and Daddy either.

Shelagh replied in a friendly way: "Just about you, I think. Anyway, Mummy sent me to fetch you."

Dusty did not move, and a wary expression settled on his face. Uncle Hank had told him he must see the captain, but he hadn't bargained for a lot of women as well.

Shelagh said reassuringly: "It's all right, you know.

I think they want to help you." She began to straighten his ruffled clothing. "They mustn't see you've been fighting."

Up in the chartroom Captain and Mrs. Ford were seated on opposite sides of the captain's big desk. The desk was covered with papers needing attention, and the captain looked rather cross. Mrs. Ford, a nice-looking, dark woman with hair fashionably dressed, and wearing a grey flannel suit with a fresh white blouse, regarded her husband with slightly raised eyebrows.

"Whatever you do, Jim, you're surely not going to send the child back to these awful people in Hull?"

"I can't keep him around the ship, my dear," said the captain impatiently.

Mrs. Ford smiled persuasively. "Not even for a few days, dear?"

The captain looked away. He knew those wheedling tones. "Not even for a few days," he replied, with more firmness than he felt.

Mrs. Ford was silent for a few moments. Then, with a speculative glance, she said softly: "We might have him home for a while. Had you thought of that?"

"I had *not*," said her husband definitely.

"I don't see why not," mused Mrs. Ford, in the tone of one who is already mentally rearranging beds and planning meals.

"It's no use being soft about the boy just because he has no parents," said the captain irritably, shifting the papers in front of him. "He's broken the law and he must take the consequences."

"Oh, Jim," reproached Mrs. Ford. "I think it shows a fine adventurous spirit. It ought to be encouraged."

The captain threw up his hands in mock despair, and

at that moment the door opened. Shelagh entered, pulling Dusty by the hand.

"Here he is, Mummy. His name's Dusty."

Dusty came forward uncertainly. The captain's back was turned to him, so that his first sight was of Mrs. Ford. She gave him a welcoming smile. Almost in spite of himself he smiled back.

"Hullo, Dusty," said Mrs. Ford in a natural sort of way. "Is that your real name?"

"No, ma'am," replied Dusty shyly. "It's Jonathan Jonathan Bates. Dusty's my nickname."

"Well, Dusty," said Mrs. Ford, with a challenging glance at the captain, "I want you to come home with us —that is, with Shelagh here, and David."

Dusty's eyes opened wide. This was the last thing he had expected. His first thought was of his Uncle Hank. This lady might be all right. She looked nice and kind. But he couldn't go and leave Uncle Hank while he was in trouble. Guardedly he asked, "Is Uncle Hank coming too?"

Mrs. Ford turned to her husband. The captain left his chair and put his hand on the boy's shoulder.

"No, Dusty. That wouldn't quite work. Besides, I can't spare him, you know."

"But——" began Dusty. And then he stopped, for he'd very nearly said something that would have given his uncle away.

"Listen, my boy," said the captain, gravely but kindly. "Your uncle has put you in my charge, and by rights I should hand you over to the police. You know that, don't you?"

Dusty hung his head.

"Yes, sir," he said in a low voice.

"Luckily for you," the captain continued, with a rueful

smile, " I'm not always master in my own ship. Mrs.
Ford wants to take you home for a few days until we can
decide what's best for you."

Dusty looked from one to another. His heart was
touched by their kindness and his voice was not quite
steady as he said: " Thank you very much, sir. I'd like
to."

" That's fine. I'll tell your uncle where you've gone,
and I dare say he'll be able to come and see you."

" Of course," agreed Mrs. Ford warmly. " Have you
got anything you want to bring with you, Dusty ?"

" My other shirt's in one of the lifeboats, ma'am. It's
quite a good one."

" Go and get it, then, and we'll all go home."

Dusty turned quickly. As he reached for the handle
the door was pushed towards him. David stood in the
opening. For a second the two eyed each other stonily;
then Dusty hurried off down the narrow corridor.

" Oh, there you are, David," said Mrs. Ford, who had
risen and was beginning to draw on her gloves. " I've
got a nice surprise for you. Dusty Bates—the boy who
just ran out—is coming to stay with us for a few days.
He'll sleep in the other bed in your room."

" I don't call it a nice surprise. I think it's a beastly
idea," said David rudely. " I won't *have* him sharing
my room. It isn't fair."

" That's enough, David," said his father sharply.
" Your mother's invited him and he's coming. He's a
very decent lad and he's been badly treated. I want you
both to be as nice as you can to him."

David flung himself into a chair and stared moodily at
his feet, refusing to notice Shelagh's sisterly grimace.
The captain sat down at his desk and began to put his
papers together. Mrs. Ford, ignoring David's outburst,

Dusty gives a Promise

said cheerfully: "We're just waiting while he fetches his things, and then we're all going home to lunch."

.   .   .   .

Dusty found his way quickly down to the deck, but as he approached the forward part of the ship he came upon a sight which brought him to a sudden stop.

The deck cargo was being shifted.

Even as he watched, the giant arm of the crane, with its pendant chain and hook, swung smoothly to rest over a packing-case lying ready in the rope cradle.

"Gosh!" thought Dusty. "That's the case with the jewels in it."

Two men sprang forward and attached the hook. The bosun signalled to the crane operator, and the case rose slowly into the air.

Dusty ran to the port rails and watched its progress. Higher and higher it rose, and then, with almost human skill, the huge arm carried its burden over the dockside and into a yawning opening on the first floor of a warehouse. Men came out of the darkness, edged the case on to a truck, and pushed it out of sight.

Dusty stood staring, all else forgotten.

A piercing blast on a steam whistle brought him to himself with a start. It was time for the midday lunch break. Instantly the air was filled with the sound of hurrying footsteps. From the ship, stevedores clattered down the shore gangways fore and aft. The few members of the crew disappeared below for their meal. Men emerged from the warehouses and streamed along the wharf. The crane came to a standstill. Its operator climbed nimbly down the steel ladder and was soon lost in the crowd. In a few moments the dock-side was empty and silent, except for the shrill cries of the hovering seagulls.

The Bellamy Jewels

Dusty turned aside and made his way to the lifeboat where he had hidden the paper carrier containing his few belongings. His thoughts were so much taken up by what he had seen that he did not notice two figures which had detached themselves from the crowd and mounted the after gangway.

Tub Timkins and the huge Walrus, for they were the two figures, halted as they reached the deck.

"Dere's Miller's nephew kid," said Walrus suddenly. He gave Tub a mighty poke in the ribs and pointed.

Tub looked round Walrus's shoulder along the empty deck. Dusty had swarmed up the davit and was busy unfastening the canvas cover of the lifeboat. Tub's expression altered. "By himself too," he murmured, his eyes narrowing.

"Vhat ve do about him, Tub?"

Tub rubbed his bristly chin with a grimy hand.

"Ask him a few question, for a *start*," he said grimly. "I'll teach him to go snooping about in the dark."

"You t'ink he see vhat happen to Ginger?"

"I dunno," said Tub. "If he did," he went on savagely, "he's got to be put where he can't talk."

A slow grin spread over Walrus's enormous face. His thick lips parted, and behind his flowing moustache could be seen jagged, discoloured teeth, like slimy green rocks curtained by seaweed. Under the lowering brows his round ape-like eyes gleamed with sudden cunning. "How about putting him dere vidout asking no questions?" he suggested avidly. "Yust in case?"

Tub regarded him with surprised approval, for something of that kind had been developing in his own mind. He gave a brief look round. There was nobody about. "Listen," he said, swiftly making up his mind. "You go ashore and keep watch."

Dusty gives a Promise

"I get you," Walrus took him up. "I go ashore. I vait. You drive him down gangway. Bingo, I clap dese hands on him"—he held out his enormous paws and made a significant gesture—"and drop him in de river. Yaas?"

"Don't be a fool," said Tub shortly. "Do as I say. Get moving."

Walrus lumbered off and Tub watched him for a moment, his eyes clearly showing the contempt he felt for Walrus's blundering methods. His own ideas were very different. Forcing a disarming smile to his face, he began to stroll in a casual fashion up the deck.

By this time Dusty had finished his task and was jumping down from the lifeboat with a paper carrier bag in his hand. He was about to make his way happily back to the bridge when he caught sight of Tub weaving towards him through the cargo.

Dusty stood transfixed, all the fear and horror of the previous night crowding back on him. In imagination he felt Tub's cruel fingers gripping his shoulders, heard his very voice. "One word from you," he'd threatened, "and I'll tear the living guts out of you." Dusty's blood chilled and he fought a rising panic. Then, as Tub came nearer, he looked again and noticed the friendly smile, the easy way of walking. Perhaps he'd been a bit mistaken. Young as he was, Dusty already knew that things always seem much worse at night. He began to breathe more freely, but all the same he edged cautiously behind a long cargo skip as Tub approached him from the other side of it. Tub's smile was even more expansive and friendly.

"I've been looking for you, Dusty," he began in an ingratiating manner.

Dusty was wary. He made no movement. "Why?" he asked.

"Message from your Uncle Hank." Tub leaned over the skip confidentially. "He's got some important news for you. He asked me to fetch you."

As he spoke, Tub began to sidle round the skip, but Dusty moved also. "Why couldn't he fetch me himself?" he asked suspiciously.

"There's no time to explain all that now," countered Tub. "Come with me," he invited easily, "and I'll tell you on the way."

Tub's manner was so plausible that Dusty wavered in his fears. Indeed, he was just about to pause in his movement and allow Tub to get to him when he saw something that set the blood chasing madly through his veins.

Over the edge of the forward gangway, not twenty yards away, peered Walrus, and one glimpse of the expression on that great brutal face left Dusty in no doubt of his peril.

By a swift movement Tub saw what he was looking at and realized his guile had failed. The false smile was swept from his face.

"Come here, you little fool," he snarled, and lunged over the skip.

Dusty dodged round the deck cargo and made a dash for the bridge companion. But he was too late. Tub's long legs got him there first and he dived forward to grab the boy.

"Leave me alone!" cried Dusty, side-stepping frantically.

Tub's hand missed him and seized on the paper carrier. The string handles tore away. Tub staggered backwards and Dusty sprang out of reach. His only course now was along the starboard side of the deckhouse. He ran madly. With an oath, Tub dashed the carrier to the deck and leapt forward in pursuit.

Dusty gives a Promise

Round the far corner of the deckhouse Dusty came full tilt to the edge of the open hold. Beyond was the bare stern-deck. No cover and no escape. He skirted the hold and found himself opposite the after gangway. If only he could keep up the pace, he could surely find some place to hide, and regain the ship later. He darted down the gangway, jumped to shore, and swerved to the right.

He had reckoned without Walrus.

The huge figure, slow to move but menacing in size, spread out its arms and barred his way. Swiftly Dusty turned about and pelted down the wharf, away from the ship.

The two men pounded after him.

Panting and frightened, Dusty glanced over his shoulder. They were gaining on him. The *Tilbury Pride* seemed miles away. By now he was abreast of another ship, with a crane ranged alongside. He dodged round a stationary lorry, hoping to cut back to safety.

Tub sped past, signalling to Walrus to cut off the boy's retreat.

Again Dusty found himself barred by the ape-like figure. Desperately he whipped round, only to find Tub ahead of him, the platform of the idle crane between them.

He was caught.

He gazed round wildly. The crane? It was his only hope. From the platform, like Jack's beanstalk, the steel ladder soared into the sky. Like a flash Dusty vaulted on to the platform and set hands and feet to the narrow rungs. In a few seconds he had reached the half-way platform. He looked down.

Tub and Walrus were at the foot of the ladder, but they seemed in no hurry. Tub pushed back his hat and leered up at him evilly. Walrus clenched a huge fist and brandished it. With a horrible sinking feeling Dusty realized that he'd made a mistake. There was no way out this time. He saw Walrus spit on his hands, grasp the ladder, and begin to mount.

Dusty turned and started on the second half of his perilous climb. His legs were trembling and he began to feel dizzy. "I mustn't look down," he told himself, fixing his eyes on the little platform at the top. At last he reached it and, hanging on to the railing, took stock of his pursuers.

Ponderously Walrus was placing one foot above the other. He did not look as though he was enjoying himself. Taking small comfort from this, Dusty darted into the cabin. Perhaps there would be something he could throw. He looked round quickly. There was only a little stool clamped to the floor in front of a large panel covered with switches, each marked for its purpose. On either side and at right angles to the panel was a viewing window.

At any other time Dusty would have been thrilled. Indeed, it flashed across his mind that only this morning he had thought what fun it would be to control a crane. The recollection, together with the vital need to take some sort of action, prompted him to turn a switch. Nothing happened. He tried another—and another. Still nothing happened. Desperately his eyes roved over the panel. Above it was a larger switch clearly marked MAIN CONTROL. Without giving himself time to think, he turned it.

Immediately there arose a strange and startling whirring noise. The cabin began to vibrate as the motor gathered speed. Dusty jumped to a window. Like the questing trunk of an elephant, the boom of the crane was moving in a majestic arc. Filled with a wild excitement, a mixture of terror and triumph, Dusty leapt back to the panel.

Dusty gives a Promise

He turned one of the smaller switches. It was marked TRACK L. The noise of the motor gathered in strength. He glanced out of the window towards the river. The ship alongside seemed to be slipping from its moorings. Dusty could hardly believe his eyes. He turned to the other window. In a dignified manner, the roofs of the warehouses were also sliding past.

"Oh crikey!" thought Dusty, "the whole thing's on the move. What shall I do?"

He stepped quickly out to the platform. Walrus was hurtling down the ladder with clumsy haste. Tub was at the foot, beckoning urgently, looking this way and that. No help there, and not another soul in sight. As he watched, Walrus reached the bottom. The two men leapt from the moving platform and ran.

Dusty felt a spasm of relief, but it was quickly banished when he looked forward. The crane was increasing in speed. Less than a ship's length away was another crane, stationary on the track. "Oh gosh!" groaned Dusty. "Why doesn't somebody come?"

He dived back into the cabin. Where was the switch he had turned before? There it was. TRACK L. Beside it was another. TRACK R. Perhaps that was the one to stop it. Frantically he snapped it over. The crane came smoothly to a standstill. But only for a moment. With a further surge of power it began to move back the way it had come.

"Help! Oh help!" cried Dusty aloud. With the recklessness of desperation, he turned every switch in sight. Surely one of them would stop this hateful monster? But no. The boom swayed this way and that. The chain cable paid out with a terrifying rattle. Paralysed with fright, Dusty clung to the cabin doorway. The huge hook was now dragging along the wharf. In its path was a wheeled loading trolley with permanent slinging tackle. The boom rose. The hook hovered over the trolley. By a chance in a thousand, it engaged with the lifting tackle. For a few yards the trolley rolled along the wharf. Then, with a capricious jerk, the boom lifted again and the trolley rose in the air.

Dusty gazed, rooted to the spot. There was something moving in the trolley. To his horror there appeared the round red face of a man in a cloth cap. Two hands came up and grasped the sides. The man's face was ludicrous in its amazement. He knelt with mouth agape. Then the boom began playfully to frolic from side to side, now high, now low.

"Help! help!" yelled the victim, as if it had suddenly come to him that this was not, after all, a lunch-time dream inspired by cheese and pickles. He tried to stand up, but a sudden swoop of the boom threw him to his knees again. His cap pitched over his nose. "Help! Murder!" he bawled. "Fred! Where are you? Cut off the power. The crane's gorn barmy!"

At last his cries caused a man to appear in the doorway of a red-brick power house which the crane was now passing. Dusty caught a brief glimpse of the man's alarmed face before he rushed back into the building.

The crane stopped abruptly with the boom poised over the river. The trolley rocked perilously. "Help! help!" roared the occupant. "I can't swim!" His shouts began to attract a crowd.

All at once it came to Dusty that he was wasting valuable time. Pretty soon they would start to investigate this erratic behaviour on the part of the crane. Unless he got away immediately, he would be in serious trouble.

He took a deep breath and summoned up all his courage. The ground looked awfully far away. Seizing hold of the

Dusty gives a Promise

handrail, he put a gingerly foot on the topmost rung of the ladder. Once more he told himself not to look down. In a few seconds he had reached the base of the crane and jumped to the ground.

He looked round cautiously. As he had foreseen, the rescuers were making for the crane. They would have to reach the cabin to lower the trolley to safety. He was only just in time. He began to run in the direction of the *Tilbury Pride*.

Hurrying towards him was a small figure in a gym tunic and blazer. It was Shelagh. From her expression it was clear that she had seen a part, at least, of his recent exploits.

"Whatever have you been doing, Dusty?" she called in an awed voice. "I've been looking everywhere for you."

Dusty caught hold of her arm. "I can't explain now," he said breathlessly. "Let's get away from here quick."

Shelagh was a sensible child. One look at Dusty's white face told her that this was no time for arguing. She fell into step and they ran as fast as their legs would carry them.

CHAPTER III

A Quarrel and an Accident

The Ford home was not very far from the docks. As the two children hurried along, Shelagh pointed out various landmarks such as the police station, the cinema, and the shop where they usually bought their sweets. Dusty answered vaguely; he was only half listening. But so much had happened in the last few hours that his mind was in a whirl, and now that the terror of that chase was over, he was struggling to sort things out. There were sure to be some awkward questions when he reached the Ford home, and he wanted to be able to answer them.

He knew that he himself was in awful danger from Tub and Walrus because of his knowledge of the jewels, but, now that he was clear of them and going to a safe home, he was mostly worried about Uncle Hank's situation. One thing was quite certain: Uncle Hank was innocent of any wrongdoing. But he had been so careful to make Dusty promise not to say a word about the jewels to Captain Ford or anybody like him, that Dusty knew it must be much, much worse for him. He told himself that he would cut out his tongue before he would tell anybody where they were—or had been.

And there was the crane business; that was going to be mighty difficult to explain. With the thought, he glanced at Shelagh. Dusty hadn't had much to do with girls, but he couldn't help feeling it was odd that she hadn't asked a lot of trying questions already. He was aware that she had been looking at him sideways quite a lot, as though she were sizing him up, but not another word had she said about the crane.

In truth, Shelagh's glances had quite another meaning. She had heard her father telling her mother about Dusty's life in Hull, and she was filled with a motherly desire to help and protect him. Also she had decided he was quite good-looking, and she began to imagine how much better he would appear in nicer clothes. She had taken to him from the moment she had first seen him standing up to the domineering David, and she was sure he would be great fun to have in their home.

She stopped suddenly on a corner. " This is our road." she told him.

A Quarrel and an Accident

Engrossed in his thoughts, Dusty had been dimly conscious that the streets through which they had passed had become progressively less grimy and less like the dockyard surroundings to which he was accustomed. Now he found himself looking down a broad, quiet road of well-kept houses which proclaimed a style of life he had never before encountered.

Shelagh felt rather proud as she saw the look of wonder in his eyes. She took his arm to hurry him along, but Dusty hung back. He was nearly there and he still hadn't made up his mind what to say if the crane was mentioned. Then he had a brainwave. Why hadn't he thought of it before? Of course, if he could prevent Shelagh from referring to it, he wouldn't need to say anything at all.

"About that crane," he began haltingly. And then, to his astonishment, Shelagh took the very words from his mouth.

"I shouldn't say anything about it if I were you," she advised him breezily. "Daddy might be cross."

Dusty gazed at her, wondering just how much she had really seen, but before he could set about finding out, she had told him all that he wanted to know.

"When I saw all those men running about and you climbing down from the crane," she went on, "I couldn't believe my eyes."

Dusty's heart lightened, for it was clear that she had only seen the end of his escapade. But he was not out of the wood yet; he had awakened Shelagh's curiosity, and, as he was to discover more and more in the days to come, she was not lightly to be put off, once her interest was aroused.

"Why did you go up there?" she asked as they walked slowly along the road.

Dusty hesitated. "I—I wanted to find out how it worked," he said at last, with a rush.

"You might have done dreadful things if you'd really got it going," she observed soberly.

"I know," gulped Dusty, thinking of the man he had nearly tipped into the river, and all the other hair-raising antics that crane had performed.

"Do you always pry into things to see how they work?" pursued Shelagh.

"Not always," he hedged.

Shelagh made a gesture he didn't understand, and spoke with a depth of feeling which surprised him.

"I wish you'd get a longing to find out how our piano works," she said, with impatient distaste, "then you might be able to do something to stop it. But," she added hastily, "you'd better not do it."

She stopped and opened a green-painted gate numbered 49 in shining brass figures. A tesselated paving of black-and-white check led up to a porch and a green-painted door. "This is our house."

Dusty followed her slowly. "I don't suppose your brother will be very pleased to see me," he remarked gloomily.

Shelagh laughed. "Oh, you don't have to worry about *him*," she said carelessly, beating a loud tattoo with the knocker. "He'll soon get over it."

Dusty stepped into the porch. There were two multi-coloured glass panels in the front door, and through them he could see a figure approaching. The door opened and Mrs. Ford, in a flowered pinafore, stood smiling down at them.

"Oh, *there* you are," she said, as though, after searching under tables, behind sofas and in cupboards, she had at last run them to earth. "Come along in, Dusty." She ran a motherly eye over him. "I expect you'd like a wash. Shelagh, take Dusty up to the bathroom and give him a clean towel. Don't be long. I'm just going to take lunch in."

Dusty stood on the front-door mat feeling rather like the Bisto kid on the advertisement hoarding, for the first thing that struck him was the delicious smell of cleanliness and flowers and, faint but enticing, the odour of good food cooking. And then he noticed the rich polish of the oak chest and the glow of a copper bowl filled with velvety scarlet blossoms splashing their colour against the cream-washed walls. He scraped his feet nervously at sight of the thick brown carpet fitted right up to the walls, and when he thought of the disorderly darkness and dreariness of the home from which he had come, he was almost ready to turn and run, for he felt like an interloper. But Mrs. Ford was smiling at him and gently urging him forward, and Shelagh was beckoning from the stairs, and shyly, as though in a dream, he followed.

When he saw the white-tiled bathroom with its immaculate bath and basin, shining chromium taps and fittings, and gaily-coloured curtains, he stood completely tongue-tied. Here was something he could never even have imagined. But Shelagh was turning on the taps and selecting a snow-white towel so casually that he could not but realize that this was nothing wonderful but just a part of her everyday life, something she took for granted. What he did not realize at that moment was how soon and how easily he, too, would accept such things as normal. He set to work vigorously with soap and nailbrush, for, indeed, he could not remember when he had last had a good wash.

During the meal the young people were rather subdued. The two boys, sitting on opposite sides of the table, avoided looking at each other, David because he was still sulking and Dusty because he was overcome by his surroundings. Shelagh, who usually kept up a lively chatter, ate her Irish stew and treacle pudding in a business-like fashion but had little to say. Mrs. Ford, supposing that they needed time to get to know one another, served the meal with cheerful efficiency and talked with the captain of her plans for his brief time at home.

"Now, David," she suggested, when the pudding dish was empty and they had all risen from the table, "why don't you take Dusty upstairs and show him some of your things?"

David gave his mother a dark look and seemed about to refuse, but he caught his father's eye, changed his mind, and moved slowly to the door. Dusty followed reluctantly. He hoped Shelagh would come too. But her mother had other ideas.

"Not you, Shelagh. Your practising first. You've been out all the morning, you know."

Shelagh scowled at the detested piano. "Oh, Mummy. Must I?"

"No arguments, Shelagh," said Mrs. Ford firmly, beginning to clear the table.

Shelagh flounced over to the piano, which stood across one side of the bay window. On the music stand was a book of scales and exercises. She began to thump them out mutinously.

The airy, cream-walled room to which David led him seemed to Dusty to be everything a boy could wish for. He would never have believed such a room could exist.

At the far end was a big bay window, on the left of which were two divan beds with their heads to the wall. Opposite to them was a large chest of drawers. On his right, as he stood by the door, was a fireplace, and beyond

A Quarrel and an Accident

that a door to a further room. Facing him was another, smaller sash window.

On cream-painted bookshelves stood rows of brightly coloured books, boxes of games and Meccano. Through the half-open door of a cupboard he could see roller skates and boxing gloves, a box of tools and a cricket bat. Laid out on the open space of floor at his feet was an electrically run model railway, with station and signal boxes, bridges and tunnels, a streamlined engine and every kind of coach.

Dusty was entranced with all he saw, but if David expected him to say so, he was going to be disappointed. For a moment the two boys stood awkwardly silent, the sound of Shelagh's stumbling scales seeming to increase the constraint between them. Then David sank to his knees by the railway and pressed down a small lever. The train began to travel swiftly and smoothly.

Dusty moved a step nearer. This was the railway of his dreams. He glanced at David, but the other boy's eyes were obstinately turned away. Dusty squatted down beside the track.

Suddenly, with a petulant gesture, David switched off the power, jumped to his feet, and left the room. Dusty heard him shouting to Shelagh to shut the dining-room door. The minutes went by and he did not return. Unable to resist the temptation, Dusty leaned forward and pressed the starting lever. As he did so, his knee touched an unnoticed switch. The train started up again. Dusty sat back on his heels, his hazel eyes glowing with pleasure. He looked up as David re-entered the room.

The older boy said nothing. Dusty fancied he looked less unfriendly. He knelt down on the floor.

" I say," began Dusty impulsively, " I've never——"

His words were cut short by a resounding crash. The

express had collided head-on with a standing goods train.
Engine and coaches lay on their backs on the carpet, their
wheels revolving helplessly.

"*Now* look what you've done!" exploded David angrily.
"You've altered the points."

"I have *not*," cried Dusty indignantly.

"You must have done. How dare you touch my
things!"

"You do make a fuss," said Dusty scornfully. "I was
only having a go."

"Well, don't do it again. It's private, see?"

Dusty's temper began to rise.

"Everything's private with you. I'm sorry I came to
your house. I can't touch a thing."

David, unmoved, switched off the power and began to
replace engine and coaches on the rails.

"Well, anyway, don't touch," he said flatly.

"Who wants to? It's a silly little train, anyway,"
jeered Dusty.

"It's the best train *you've* ever seen."

This was too near the truth to be allowed to pass.

"I've seen one twice as big as that. *And* I've seen
things a heap better than anything you've got."

Dusty rose to his feet and looked round the room
disparagingly. David rose also.

"I bet you haven't," he retorted.

"Yes, I have."

"I bet you haven't seen a real sextant or a chrono
meter."

"Of *course* I have. My Uncle Hank gave me one,"
said Dusty defiantly.

"That's good, I must say," sneered David. "Your
Uncle Hank! Why, even captains don't have private
ones—only my father."

A Quarrel and an Accident

"Where is it, then?" challenged Dusty. "Show it to me."

David paused. The two boys measured glances. Then David threw back his head with sudden reckless resolve. "All right," he said loftily. "Wait here a minute."

He went to the door and listened. There was only the sound of Shelagh's exercises and the distant rattle of crockery from the kitchen. But the pause gave David time to think, and he was suddenly appalled at what he was going to do. The chronometer was on the mantel-piece in his father's room. It was about the most sacred thing in the house, and nobody, not even his mother, was allowed to lay a finger on it. If his father came up and saw him carrying it, David did not know what would happen. He almost drew back and gave up the idea, but he knew that Dusty's eyes were on him; he simply must go on. He set his teeth and went out. Dusty saw him enter a room across the landing and a few seconds later he came back, holding in both hands a heavy instrument in a polished wooden case with a glass face.

"If my father knew I was showing you this, he'd have a fit."

"I don't think much of it," said Dusty, unimpressed. "It's only an old clock."

"Don't you know *anything*?" complained David, his exasperation increased by his knowledge of wrongdoing. "This is worth a stack of money. Open the back and look inside, *then* you'll see something."

Clumsily he reversed the instrument so that the back was uppermost. Dusty fumbled with the catch.

"Not that way, silly," said David impatiently, for any moment his father might come in. "Turn the knob and pull."

Dusty obeyed. The little door remained fast. "Harder,"

urged David. Dusty gave it a violent tug. It opened
suddenly. David's foot slipped. He tried to recover his
balance. The instrument fell from his hands and struck
the floor with a dull thud.

David gazed down at it, horrified. It was the most
awful thing that had ever happened in his whole life.

Captain Ford, reading his newspaper in the dining-
room below, raised his head sharply and looked at the
ceiling. Shelagh's hands dropped from the piano keys.
She twisted round on the stool.

" What was that, Shelagh?"

" I don't know, Daddy," replied Shelagh uncertainly.

" Better go and see, I suppose," muttered her father,
throwing his newspaper aside and striding from the room.

Dusty was now standing alone in the playroom, the
chronometer still face downwards at his feet. He heard
the captain mounting the stairs two at a time, and a feeling
of panic came over him. The footsteps crossed the landing
and the captain appeared in the doorway. His eyes went
swiftly from Dusty's guilty figure to the chronometer
on the floor. An expression of cold anger spread over his
handsome, clean-shaven face. He came forward and
picked up the instrument. The little door was torn
from its hinges; the glass face was cracked.

" What is the meaning of this?" he inquired with
terrifying calm.

Dusty felt the blood drain from his face. He clenched
his hands, trying to hide their trembling. He did not
know what to say. At last he stammered: " It—it—
slipped, sir."

" *Slipped?*" repeated the captain, icily incredulous.
" What were you doing with it?"

Dusty dared not look at him.

" I—I—was l-looking inside, sir."

A Quarrel and an Accident

" How did you get hold of it ? "

Dusty made no reply. He glanced at the door of the inner room and thought contemptuously of David, who had run away.

" You've broken something I value more than anything I possess," said the captain, with bitter reproach. " You see that ? " He pointed to an engraved plate. Dusty read confusedly : " Presented to Captain James Ford for great gallantry at sea." He was very near to tears. " And you had to smash it to see inside. I'm very disappointed in you.".

Carrying the chronometer, the captain left the room and went downstairs.

Dusty was used to flaming rages, wild words and blows. It was the first time he had ever experienced the controlled anger that expresses itself in a few searing words, and somehow it seemed to shrivel him up. He had a horrible feeling that he had shrunk to a smaller size, and had become something that was infinitely contemptible.

Then he saw David looking out from the doorway of the other room into which he had retreated. This was Shelagh's room, but Dusty didn't know it then. His eyes blazed with indignant wrath as he glanced at David, but he judged from his attitude that David was feeling pretty small too. His hands were thrust into his trousers pockets and his head slumped forward. He just stood in the doorway and didn't speak. Dusty curled his lips and turned his back.

In the dining-room Mrs. Ford was arranging some chrysanthemums in a vase on the table. Shelagh sat at the piano, vaguely turning over the pages of her exercise book. The captain entered and put the chronometer down on the table. At sight of his set face Mrs. Ford exclaimed : " Oh, Jim ! Whatever's happened ? "

"I found Dusty Bates in the playroom with this on the floor at his feet," said the captain grimly.

"Oh, *darling*. I'd rather *anything* had been broken than that."

"I'm afraid we've made a mistake, my dear," said the captain, his anger now tinged with regret. "This boy has no respect for property. Perhaps this will give you an idea of what we are up against."

Mrs. Ford looked distressed. "Poor little boy," she said pityingly. "It's his upbringing, I suppose."

"We can't be responsible for that. No, Mary," he went on firmly, "I hate to go against your wishes, but I don't think we can go on looking after him. We shall have to take the other course after all."

Shelagh, who had been listening to her parents with her eyes wide, now jumped from her stool and came to the table.

"Oh, Daddy!" she cried, "does that mean you're going to send him away?"

The captain nodded his head. "I'm afraid so, Shelagh."

Shelagh looked tragically from him to her mother. "Oh, *Mummy*!" she exclaimed, and dashed from the room and up the stairs.

When she entered the playroom, David was standing by the side window fiddling aimlessly with the wooden acorn on the end of the blind cord. He did not look at her. She went straight up to Dusty, who was sitting forlornly on one of the beds. He rose to his feet.

"Dusty, *why* did you touch that clock?" she burst out passionately. "Daddy's simply furious. He's going to send you away."

"I was going to run away, anyhow," replied Dusty stonily.

A Quarrel and an Accident

" But why did you *touch* the clock?" persisted Shelagh vehemently.

Dusty said nothing. Shelagh turned accusingly to David.

" You knew. You should have stopped him."

There was silence. Shelagh looked from one to the other, a dawning suspicion in her clear grey eyes. David's face had gone very pink. She waited. At last, with a sort of shamed defiance, David said: " I got it from Daddy's room to show him. We both dropped it—and I'm going to tell Father."

" David!" exclaimed Shelagh, her voice shrill with indignation. " I should just think you would!"

When David opened the dining-room door, Mrs. Ford was saying: " I can't understand it, Jim. He seemed such a nice boy."

The captain shrugged his shoulders, and then, seeing David and mistaking his errand, he said rather irritably: " It's no use looking so glum, my boy. I've made up my mind. He's going."

" But, Dad," blurted out David, " it was my fault. I got the clock and we dropped it when we were—trying to open it."

" I see," said the captain slowly, and David quailed under the chilly blue eyes.

" *You* got the chronometer from my room?" queried the captain. His voice was very quiet, but the simple, direct words had a stabbing quality.

" Yes."

" And *you* helped to smash it?"

David could only nod his drooping head. Mrs. Ford watched in a hushed sort of way.

" I like people to look into my face when I am speaking," his father reminded him, still in the same quiet tones.

With an effort David forced himself to look up; and it was an effort, not so much for fear of his father's face as for shame of himself.

"And where were you when I came up?" demanded the captain sternly.

"In Shelagh's room."

"Why?"

David wriggled miserably; then he steeled himself and met his father's eyes firmly.

"I funked," he confessed simply, and waited, without flinching. But he saw a new light flicker in his father's eyes at this, and when the captain next spoke his voice had a kindlier quality.

"That's more like the boy I know," he approved, and added, quite gently: "Everybody makes mistakes in conduct, but those who are worth while realize it and waste no time in owning up."

David heard his mother breathe a sigh of relief, and as his father began to smile at him, a lump came to his throat. He felt suddenly weak and silly, and detested it. He was conscious of a strange flash of resentment too. It wasn't fair that his weaknesses should be exposed in this way and then forgiven so understandingly. It made him feel small—and foolish. He dashed the back of his hand across his eyes.

Captain Ford reached out and put an arm round his shoulders, and as he was drawn close to his father's side, David was glad of the chance to cover his face.

"I know how you feel, David," the captain said, almost confidentially. "But think about Dusty Bates. What strikes me is, that boy didn't split. Did you notice that?"

David had noticed, and he made it clear that he had. And after that Captain Ford, as usual, did not make the mistake of saying too much. He merely remarked: "I should go up and be a bit decent to him, if I were you. It will make you feel better."

David couldn't trust himself to speak. He pulled away and left the room. But he lingered quite a while on the stairs, for he had plenty to think about.

In the sitting-room, the captain began to charge his pipe happily.

"And that's that," he remarked, with a smile of content.

Mrs. Ford was still looking at him. "It's worth having something broken, just to see the way you behave, Jim," she said softly, and the feeling in her eyes did not want much divining.

The captain was looking at the chronometer. He pretended to be wry, but he was smiling. "Maybe it isn't broken beyond repair after all," he said reflectively.

"I do hope so, I'm sure," murmured Mrs. Ford, her thoughts beginning to turn elsewhere. She went out into the hall, and the captain smiled as he heard her ordering Shelagh to come down and finish her practising.

"That girl would do anything rather than practise," she grumbled, as she returned, "but I've paid for her lessons and she's going to be able to play, whether she likes it or not."

Shelagh came in, rebellious and frowning, and began to thump the keys. Her father made a protesting face and puffed an indignant cloud of smoke.

"You haven't paid me to listen," he told his wife, and he would have left the room, but just then the telephone bell rang.

Shelagh promptly stopped playing and listened idly as her father took the call. She supposed it was just some matter connected with the ship, and prepared to let her thoughts wander pleasantly. But in a moment she sat up and listened attentively, for it was evidently something to do with Dusty.

Although Shelagh didn't know it, the caller was Detective-Inspector White, and he was inquiring about Dusty at the request of the Hull police, to whom the Huggins's had reported his disappearance.

Shelagh followed the conversation as well as she could, but it was awkward hearing only one side of it. She heard her father tell the person at the other end that Dusty was safe with them. He followed this with a few guarded remarks about the Huggins's being unfit to have a boy in their charge, and then Shelagh lost interest because the talk drifted to something about jewels. But she did prick up her ears a bit when Hank Miller's name was mentioned, and she wondered why her father was so insistent about Hank's good character, and why he asserted so positively that Miller was one of his most reliable men.

But Shelagh was not to know that the inquiries were caused by the Hull police, who were still trying to trace the jewels, and as the captain ended the conversation just then, she proceeded at once to try to find out why Dusty's name had been mentioned.

" Do those people want to get Dusty back?" she asked.

" They're not going to," asserted her father, as he sat down and relighted his pipe.

" What was that talk about jewels?" asked Mrs. Ford, mystified.

" I haven't told you about that," replied the captain. He glanced meaningly towards Shelagh, for he did not like to talk of things connected with crime before the children.

" Shelagh, you can go up and play with the boys," said Mrs. Ford, who was intrigued by the mention of jewels; " I can see that you've not got your mind on your music."

As Shelagh ran out, they smiled at each other, and the captain began to give an outline of what had happened after Detective-Inspector White boarded the *Tilbury Pride*.

By the time that Shelagh bounded joyfully into the bedroom, the two boys were on the best of terms, for in the interval David had demonstrated that he was only too eager to make amends. He had shown Dusty all his possessions and had given him the free run of the place and all it contained. They had just unearthed David's boxing gloves, and David, who had had some lessons at school, was trying to initiate Dusty.

Shelagh sniffed in a superior way because she didn't think much of boxing, but she couldn't help being amused when, each time David showed Dusty the proper way to guard, he received a smart bang on the nose.

" You keep punching the wrong way," objected David, rather nettled. " You aren't supposed to hit like that when I guard like this." And as he guarded by suiting the action to the word, sure enough Dusty dealt him another blow on the nose.

Shelagh grinned. In her secret heart she was glad to see David taken down a peg or two. She considered he was inclined to think a bit too much of himself, and the treatment he was getting might do him good.

" Show him again, David," she requested, with deceptive encouragement. But David was well aware of Shelagh's little ways. He pulled off his gloves.

" I'll show you another time," he promised grumpily, " when there aren't any girls about to spoil it."

Shelagh scorned to take up the challenge. She turned gaily to Dusty, who was also removing his gloves.

" I've just been hearing about you on the phone," she

told him. " The police at Hull have been asking where
you are. But it's all right," she added quickly, as Dusty's
face fell. " Daddy said those people aren't fit to have
you. That means you are going to stay here."

Dusty was reassured, but as he was replacing the
gloves in the cupboard where they were kept, Shelagh
made a further remark which went through him like an
electric shock.

" They were speaking about your Uncle Hank too," she
said off-handedly, " and there was some funny talk about
somebody's jewels."

Shelagh was surprised at the way Dusty swung round
on this.

" What did they say about them?" he asked anxiously.

" I don't know," she replied. " I only heard what
Daddy said at this end."

" What did he say?" insisted Dusty.

" He only said how well he knew your uncle, and
how reliable he is." She broke off. " Why, you look quite
frightened, Dusty. What's the matter?"

Dusty perceived that he had nearly given himself away.
David was eyeing him curiously too. But hearing that
the police had been asking about Uncle Hank in connexion with those jewels had been almost too much for
him. He determined to be more careful. First of all, he
must dispel the inquisitive wonder in both their eyes, but
the worst of it was he couldn't think of anything just right
to say on the spur of the moment, and they were both
looking at him expectantly.

He tried to pass it off by saying: " I thought at first
that you said they were talking about Uncle Hank and
his jewels." But at once he realized with dismay that he
had made another mistake, for David's eyes opened in
astonishment.

A Quarrel and an Accident

" D'you mean to say your Uncle Hank has got some jewels—real ones?" he asked.

" Of course he hasn't," Dusty denied hastily.

" But you seemed to speak as if he had," Shelagh pointed out.

Dusty began to feel more and more uncomfortable. Shelagh seemed to sense something and, even in the middle of his agitation, he made up his mind he'd be very careful what he said to her in future. Girls were evidently something to be reckoned with. And why had he been such a fool as to mention the word jewels at all? They were waiting for an answer.

" I only thought you said that," he told Shelagh touchily.

" But," she persisted, " supposing so—why should it make you so frightened?"

Would the subject never be dropped, Dusty thought wildly. But, although he didn't understand the subtle change in Shelagh's expression at this moment, David did, and he came to the rescue.

" Don't answer her, Dusty," he advised, mutely daring Shelagh. " She thinks she's got you rattled, and she's seeing how far she can go. You don't know women like I do," he added feelingly.

" Pig!" remarked Shelagh disdainfully. Then, looking round as if nothing had happened: " What shall we do? Let's try who can tell the biggest whopper."

" That only leads to arguments about who's won," asserted David. " Let's take the model boat down to the canal."

" There's no fun in that," grumbled Shelagh, " except for you."

For some time they continued, one suggesting and the other objecting, and Dusty was only too glad that he wasn't called upon to join in, for deep down inside he was in a panic. That remark about the police and Uncle Hank and the jewels had dropped among his thoughts like a bomb. He tried to think while they talked, and as he did so one thought became more and more urgent. He ought to let Uncle Hank know. He *must* let Uncle Hank know.

Just then David broke in on his thoughts. "We're going to the canal after all," he announced.

"Where is it?" asked Dusty.

"Only about ten minutes' walk."

Dusty felt his way carefully. "I've got a feeling that I'd like to see my Uncle Hank," he said, as casually as he could. "But I don't know where to find him."

"He'll be living in the Company's seamen's hostel," David said. "But can't you see him another time?"

Dusty saw that David was bent on having his own way, and this time he was grateful to Shelagh, who said: "It's natural for him to want to see his uncle, if he's very fond of him, David."

"I am," declared Dusty.

Then David made it awkward again.

"All right," he gave in, "we'll go that way to the canal and see him with you."

"I'd rather see him alone," said Dusty quickly, and Shelagh, seeing his troubled face, came to his aid again.

"Don't be so bossy, David," she said. "Let Dusty do as he likes." She turned to Dusty. "You'll just have time before tea."

She ran her eye over him in motherly fashion, made a mental note to ask her mother to let him have one of David's suits before he went out next time, and gave him careful directions to find the hostel.

"You're sure you'll be all right out by yourself in a

strange place?" she asked finally. And Dusty, eager to get to Hank, reassured her and left.

Dusty crept down the stairs. He could hear the voices of Captain and Mrs. Ford in the dining-room, but fortunately the door was closed. He tiptoed down the passage to the rear of the house and found himself in the kitchen. Closing the door carefully behind him, he moved across to the back door, which opened on to a little paved yard formed by the scullery, which stood out at right angles to the kitchen, and by the brick wall which separated No. 49 from the house next door.

Dusty crossed this yard diagonally, opened the back gate, and walked quietly down the tradesmen's entrance. There was a privet hedge running alongside the front garden to the fence, and here Dusty ducked down in its shelter in case Captain or Mrs. Ford was looking out of the dining-room window. He gained the pavement safely, however, and ran quickly up the street to the main road, where he turned to the right.

Here there were trams and shops and people, and Dusty slowed down and went over in his mind the directions Shelagh had given him. Turn to the right and keep on until you see the Roxy Cinema on the other side of the road. There it was, a lavish imitation of a Moorish palace, its twin minarets incongruous amid the smoke-blackened roofs of dockland. He crossed the road and skirted the cinema. Turn left by the cinema, she'd said, and keep on past the Bull's Head till you see a street on the other side called Chandlers' Market.

Dusty hurried along. The Bull's Head was easily identified by a newly-painted sign depicting a bull of ferocious aspect. A little farther along, on the other side of the road, he could see the beginning of a very busy street towards which all the women with shopping baskets seemed to be drawn. When he got near enough he looked for the name and, as he'd expected, it was called Chandlers' Market.

Chandlers' Market had once been a street of respectable small shops serving a local population of moderately well-to-do families, but, as the docks spread farther and farther, the neighbourhood declined, and one by one the respectable tradesmen departed, giving place to cheapjack vendors whose goods overflowed vulgarly on to the pavement, and who deafened the passer-by with loud cries extolling the superiority of their wares.

As if this confusion was not enough, on certain days of the week other worthies arrived with awninged stalls which they erected in the gutter on either side, and loaded with cheap china, glassware, stockings, boots and shoes, underwear, second-hand furniture, goldfish in bowls, and cages of yapping puppies and mewing kittens. In due season mussels and winkles, roast chestnuts and hot potatoes made their appearance; in fact, you could buy almost anything from a thimble to an elephant in Chandlers' Market and, if the cries of the sellers could be believed, every article dirt cheap.

To-day was a market day, and as Dusty threaded his way down the centre of the street, he was fascinated by this colourful display and the lively Cockney back-chat between seller and buyer; he thought that he must come again another day when he had more time. But now he had a most urgent mission to carry out and, nearing the end of the street, he began to look out for the opening on the left with three iron posts which Shelagh had told him about. Yes, there it was; and there was the sign on the wall which read " Archers Court, leading to Old Dock Alley ".

Shelagh had told him that the hostel was in Old Dock

A Quarrel and an Accident

Alley, and when he came to it round the corner Dusty
thought it was about the most gloomy place he had ever
seen. It wasn't exactly an alley, it was a cobbled road.
On one side were the forbidding stone wall backs of great
warehouses; on the other was a line of large old-fashioned
houses which had been turned into storehouses. There
didn't seem to be a single house with anybody living in
it or, indeed, anybody about at all, and, after the cheerful
hurly burly of the market, Dusty found the silence rather
sinister.

As he hesitated, a horse-drawn railway van came out
of a narrow side street. The driver slowed up when Dusty
called to him, and he learned that the hostel was about
half-way down. It turned out to be just another shabby,
tumbledown house. A broken iron fence lined the footpath, and the filigree iron gate, which had rusted off its
hinges, lay among the weeds and thistles of what had
once been the front garden. A stone path led to a flight
of stone steps ascending to a shabby, unused-looking front
door.

Standing on the pavement, Dusty let his eyes roam
over the face of the building, and what he saw filled him
with misgiving. Surely Uncle Hank couldn't be living
in a place like this? Sailors had everything shipshape,
hadn't they? Nevertheless, a skew-wise board above the
pillared porch told him that this was the Ixion Steamship
Company's Hostel for Seamen, though it appeared that
only the lower half of the house was used for this purpose
because the upstairs windows were all boarded up.

The whole place looked so squalid and deserted on
this dull afternoon that Dusty, even though he was not
unused to grim surroundings, had some qualms about
going in. But it was no use hanging back, he must find
Uncle Hank; so he forced himself up the front path.

The Bellamy Jewels

And then he saw that there was a small notice-board fixed to the left-hand stone pillar at the foot of the steps. It bore the one word HOSTEL and an arrow pointing downwards and to the side. Dusty looked down and saw that there was another flight of steps leading downwards.

He moved over to some railings which surrounded the basement area and saw that below there was another door and two sash windows, the lower halves of which had been whitewashed. The upper halves were so dirty and the room inside was so dark that they merely gave back the reflection of his legs and feet between the railings. The whole place sent a damp chill through Dusty, but he knew he must go on. He began to descend the steps.

Half-way down, a horrifying thought suddenly flashed across his mind. If Uncle Hank lived here, the others would be here too—Tub and Walrus. The idea nearly sent him rushing back up the steps, but he controlled himself. It was silly, he told himself, because there didn't seem to be anybody around at all. He reached the bottom of the steps and began to try to find a scratch in the whitewash where he could see into the room. And just then his hair seemed to rise up on his head and his blood froze.

Something was touching his legs.

For a moment Dusty was so petrified with fright that he could not move. Then, as he waited with staring eyes for something awful to happen, he heard a familiar rhythmic noise, and he almost laughed out loud, for what he heard was the purring of a cat.

He looked down behind him and there, clawing at his trousers to attract attention, was a lean and scarred but exceedingly friendly old black cat.

Dusty bent down and stroked it, and the cat arched its back and pranced to and fro against his legs as though

A Quarrel and an Accident

it was many a long day since it had received so much notice. Somehow the companionship, even of a cat, was very comforting and Dusty felt much bolder. He soon found a clear spot in the whitewashed window and peered through into the murky dayroom which we have seen before. The plates and cups still littered the dirty table, but Dusty hardly noticed this, for his excited eyes had seen something else.

Uncle Hank's pea-jacket and peaked cap were lying on a form. He knew it was Uncle Hank's jacket because it had one odd and rather large brass button which was clearly visible.

Dusty's spirits lightened still more for, of course, this meant that Uncle Hank was within, and if that was so it didn't matter a bit if Tub and Walrus were there as well.

He pressed down the latch of the door and entered. The cat followed him.

Once inside, Dusty's first thought was to call out, but something stopped him. The atmosphere was stale with tobacco smoke and the odour of past meals, and it seemed heavy with silence. Then Dusty listened acutely. What was that low, muffled sort of noise? It came from somewhere at the back.

. He crept round the table and across to a door on which was painted the word DORMITORY. He pushed open the door and peeped through into a dark passage. The noise was louder, and now he could tell what it was. Somebody was snoring. He passed through into the passage and the old cat followed him.

The noise came from behind a door a little way down on the right. Dusty opened it very quietly and went in, but he was careful to leave the door open behind him. The cat looked in inquisitively and decided to follow.

The Bellamy Jewels

It was darker still in here, and after a few seconds Dusty saw that a blanket had been fastened over the window, but just enough light came in from the dim passage to enable him to make out that two of the walls were lined with bunks, very much like the fo'c'sle of the *Tilbury Pride*.

The snoring came from one of the bunks on the right-hand wall, and Dusty tiptoed across, expecting to see the features of Uncle Hank. What he did see made him gasp and his heart nearly stopped beating.

It was Tub. He smelt of beer, and his thin lips puffed in and out foolishly as he snored.

Dusty drew back terrified, and just then a great hand gripped him from above by the back of the neck and another great hand was clapped over his mouth. He looked up and saw in the semi-darkness the hideous, grinning features of Walrus. He struggled madly, but he was held as though in a vice.

" Vake up, Tub," rumbled the grinning Walrus. " Ve got a visitor."

Tub sat up with a jerk and blinked.

" It's Hank's nephew kid," boomed Walrus joyfully, " and now p'raps ve got him proper dis time. Yaas?"

Tub's response surprised Dusty. It surprised Walrus even more. For Tub's thoughts moved nimbly, and he saw possibilities that would never occur to the thick-headed giant, whose hairy paws still gripped the struggling boy.

" Lay off, you big boob," he ordered. He swung his legs over the side of the bunk and stood up. Dusty noted that he was fully dressed.

Walrus relaxed his grip and Dusty stumbled back, rubbing his hand across his mouth.

" What are you doing here, boy?" inquired Tub, and,

A Quarrel and an Accident

to Dusty's astonishment, his voice was quite mild and friendly.

" I want to see Uncle Hank," Dusty replied cautiously. You never knew where you were with Tub, but this seemed a fairly safe answer.

" Ho-ho!" jeered Walrus. " He vant to see Hank, and Hank away all dressed up in shore togs. P'raps he never see Hank again, eh, Tub?"

" Shut up, you big fool," Tub snapped viciously. " Come out here."

He grabbed Walrus by the arm and they went out. Dusty heard the key grate in the lock.

Left to himself, he saw what an idiot he had been. He might have known that Uncle Hank would change his clothes ashore. And he had been certain that he was here just because he saw his pea-jacket lying out there. The cat rubbed against his legs and he stroked it absently.

Outside in the dayroom, Tub was telling the wooden-headed Walrus a few home truths.

" But vhat's it matter, Tub, now ve got him?" protested Walrus in an aggrieved tone.

" Matter?" groaned Tub. " He's gone to live in the skipper's house, hasn't he? He's had time to talk, hasn't he? How do we know how much he's told already?"

" Den ve get rid of him before he have time to tell some more—isn't it?"

Tub made an exasperated gesture. " What's the good of making it worse by getting rid of him if he's told enough to set the others after us, mug?" he retorted. " And just when there's a chance of a bit of crafty winkling, you go and frighten the willies out of him."

" All right, all right," Walrus conceded sulkily. " P'raps you do it your vay."

In the gloom of the dormitory Dusty sat miserably on

the edge of a bunk while the old cat explored something of interest beneath. Once again he had walked into a trap and, far from helping Uncle Hank, he was in dire need of help himself.

The key rattled in the lock, and he got up as Tub opened the door and entered. For a moment he had a wild impulse to make a dash for it, but he knew it was hopeless, for he would never get past both of them. Tub left the door open, and Dusty could hear the sounds of clumsy movements as Walrus began to clear the table.

Tub was smiling agreeably. " So you came to see your uncle?" he remarked, taking a cigarette from a packet and lighting it. " I expect I shall come across him later. Is there anything you want him to know?"

Dusty thought rapidly. This was an idea. There was no reason why he shouldn't tell Tub what he had come to tell Uncle Hank, because Tub and Walrus were even deeper in the jewel business than Uncle Hank. And if, so far as he could make out, Uncle Hank would be in trouble if they got in trouble, by the same reasoning Uncle Hank would escape if they escaped. Dusty decided to chance it, and for the moment to forget his own position.

In a few words he repeated to Tub what Shelagh had told him of her father's conversation on the telephone. Tub listened intently and asked a number of careful questions. When Dusty had answered these, and thereby given Tub exactly what he knew, Tub seemed to spend some time thinking it all out.

At last he appeared to have reached a conclusion, for he said: " I don't think we need worry. It would only be routine inquiries, and they won't lead the police far. Unless you have helped," he added, with a sharp look at Dusty.

" Me?" said Dusty.

A Quarrel and an Accident

" I mean by something you've said at the skipper's house," explained Tub.

" I haven't said a word about the jewels, or anything," declared Dusty hotly. " How could I when I knew it would get Uncle Hank in trouble?"

While he spoke, Tub watched as though he could pierce through to the very centre of Dusty's brain, and from his next remark it was evident that he was satisfied by what he saw.

" You're a sensible boy," he remarked, moving. And Dusty, who was almost led away by his confidential manner, asked eagerly, " Can I go now?"

Just for an instant Dusty had the impression that a queer cunning look drifted across Tub's face, but he must have been mistaken, he decided, because Tub's reply showed the utmost concern for his welfare.

" You stay here and keep quiet till I get a chance to let you out," he advised. " I have to be careful with Walrus because he's a nasty customer when he's upset."

Dusty had no difficulty in believing this.

Tub went to the door. " Wait here, and don't make any fuss," he urged again.

With a sinking heart, Dusty again heard the lock grating home, and his disquiet was increased because he thought that that crafty look had reappeared on Tub's face as he left the room. He stood watching the door helplessly for a moment, then he caught the mutter of words, and he realized that the door into the dayroom had been left open. He crossed to the locked door and pressed his ear tight up against it.

In the dayroom, Walrus had cleared the table and was slicing some rashers from an odd-shaped piece of bacon. Tub entered swiftly. " He hasn't said a word," he exulted in his soft voice.

Walrus's response was loud and clear. " Den he don't get no more chance to talk, eh, Tub?" he boomed. " Ve got him proper. Yaas?"

He gleefully sliced off a rasher and slapped it into the frying-pan beside him. " Smack, like dat!" He sliced another rasher and repeated the action. " And smack, like dat!" Then he paused and his voice sank to a conspira-torial level.

" How ve go about it, Tub?"

Tub made a horrifying gesture. " But first of all," he said, " we wait till it's dark. He'll keep safe enough in there and he won't make any fuss." He smiled to himself as he recollected this piece of artfulness.

Walrus was silent for a moment while he savoured the import of Tub's last remarks. Then, as the possibilities came home to him, he burst out with noisy enthusiasm: " Yaas, and vhen it's dark," he bellowed, " ve drop him in river, between de ship and de vall, vhere dey von't know how he got dere, if dey find him. Yaas?"

Tub frowned. " You said that before," he observed.

" Yaas," roared Walrus. " But dis time ve done it!" He picked up the frying-pan and crossed to the gas ring. " Now ve cook and eat."

In the dormitory, Dusty, still with his ear to the door, realized that the conversation had come to an end. In any event, he had heard enough to send a sick fear shuddering to his heart. He thought about shouting and banging to attract attention, but then he remembered the deserted street and the empty houses. No matter how much noise he made, nobody would hear, except those two fiends in the next room, and he dare not think what action they might take.

His mind turned to the possibility of Uncle Hank or Squeaky turning up. But he wasn't sure that Squeaky

A Quarrel and an Accident

even stayed here, and as for Uncle Hank, they must know he wouldn't be coming back yet by the way they were preparing. He thought of the *Tilbury Pride* lying up against the wharf wall, and of what they intended to do, and it made him shake with terror. He must *do* something before his thoughts became too much for him.

He tried the door, even though he knew it was locked, just for something to do. Then he crossed to the window and pulled back the blanket. But the window was close-barred with strong round iron. Even if he tore the blanket away and opened the window, he could see by the way the bars were set in the masonry that there was no hope in this direction.

Then he examined the walls and even cast eyes at the ceiling. But there was no sign of another way out. In fact, the side wall away from the bunks was bare except for some torn old oilskins hanging on a nail. They were smothered in dust and set in stiff folds, as though they had been there for years. Dusty concluded that they had been left behind by some member of another Ixion Line crew.

Suddenly a ray of light shot through the gloom of his thoughts. Shelagh and David knew where he had gone! When he didn't come back, they would be sure to tell the captain. They might even come looking for him themselves. But his hopes sank again at once. Supposing they did? He was so far away from the entrance that he wouldn't even hear them. In fact, he wouldn't know if they had been at all, for Tub and Walrus would see them all right, and he knew what they would say. They would deny that he had ever been near the place. Dusty had a horrible sinking feeling. There was nothing he could do —nothing at all, but wait.

He sat down on the edge of a bunk and began to think

of the Fords, of Hull and the Hugginses, of Uncle Hank,
and, indeed, of everything that had ever happened in his
life. Suppose, he kept thinking, nothing at all ever happens
in my life again? He shuddered and felt that he was going
to cry. Perhaps he would have done so if the cat, at that
moment, had not decided to come out from under the
bunk.

Dusty reached down to stroke it. The cat arched its
back but it was only in a half-hearted sort of way, as if it
had lost interest in him and was intent on something else.
Dusty picked it up, but evidently it didn't feel like being
picked up, for it struggled and jumped down again. It
seemed to want something. It seemed to want something
for, after looking into Dusty's face and uttering a querulous
cry, it raised its tail and waved it from side to side as if
irritated by his lack of comprehension.

Then it stalked slowly across to the door, and now
there was no mistaking what it wanted, for it reached up
against the closed door with its forefeet and looked back
at him, but Dusty felt too miserable to try to make the
animal understand that he also wanted to get out of this
room, but couldn't.

The cat pawed at the door and looked appealingly at
Dusty a few times, but in the end it seemed to accept the
futility of trying to deal with poor things like human
beings, and sat down.

For a few moments it licked at an awkward spot behind
its shoulder which made an urgent call for grooming.
Then it got up and made unhesitatingly for the side wall,
as though it had suddenly remembered something.

Dusty watched it dully, too much absorbed in his own
dreary thoughts to take much notice, but he began to
wonder dimly what the cat was up to now, for it reached
up the wall and began nosing among the old oilskins.

A Quarrel and an Accident

Dusty couldn't make it out. But the cat was so persistent that he thought perhaps a mouse had got into one of the pockets. Merely to pass the time, he decided to have a look. And when he moved the oilskins his heart took a great jump, for there was the answer to all his troubles.

As we have already related, Dusty was fond of cats and had studied their ways. He knew that there is no limit to the ingenuity they can display where their freedom is in jeopardy, and the truth of the matter flashed into his mind at once. This old cat was evidently a resident of some long standing and knew every nook and corner. When it found that it couldn't leave the room by the door, it remembered another way that it had used at some time in the past. And there was this other way under Dusty's excited eyes; a hatchway that had long been covered by the old oilskins. It slid open at his touch, revealing a small empty room on the other side. Dusty poked his head through.

The door of this other room was open and he could see through to a passage, where there was another door which looked as though it might lead to the outside. Although it did not occur to Dusty to figure it out, this other small room, in the long-ago days when this was a large residential house, had been a pantry, and the present seamen's dormitory had been a large stillroom, and that is how the hidden hatch came to be there.

But Dusty didn't stop to consider the whys and wherefores. He could hear heavy movements from the other room and Walrus's loud voice telling Tub that he was going to have a look-see at the nephew kid. The cat had already leaped through the hatch and vanished. Dusty scrambled after it and ran across into the passage.

There was an enormous rusty key in the lock of the outer door, and he had quite a struggle to turn it; and then the door seemed to be stuck; but at last it gave with a loud report, and he found himself looking out into another basement area. He dashed up some cracked and moss-covered steps and was confronted by a wilderness of weeds and overgrown bushes and trees, at the end of which he could just make out a sagging and derelict wooden fence.

Dusty plunged into this jungle, and in a few moments had vaulted over the fence and into a long alley with a wooden fence on either side. He ran as fast as his legs would go and came out among some warehouses. He had no idea where he was, but he didn't stop to take any bearings; he just kept running until he tore round a sharp corner by a tobacconist's shop and ran full tilt into a policeman.

" Here-ere-ere!" exclaimed the surprised constable, his dignity somewhat impaired, " what's all this?"

Dusty was panting with the haste he had made. " I— I'm running because I'm late for tea," he gasped. It was the first thing that came into his head.

To the policeman, who had just come on duty after a substantial meal of fried herrings and endless cups of strong tea, it evidently seemed that Dusty's anxiety about his tea was somewhat overdone. " Where do you live?" he asked, fixing him with a suspicious gaze.

This put Dusty in a quandary because, although he knew well enough where he lived, he had forgotten to ask the name of the street. Suppose he told the policeman a silly thing like that, and the policeman insisted on going with him to see that he was telling the truth, what would he say to Captain and Mrs. Ford?

Fortunately for Dusty, at this moment the policeman's attention was distracted by the sight of a barrow of oranges which its owner had illegally allowed to come to rest while he served a customer. Dusty dodged round behind the officer of the law and sped away up the street. At the end was a main road, and on the other side he recognized delightedly the fiery eye and distended nostrils of the painted bull on the sign of the Bull's Head.

As he approached the corner of Beverley Road, Dusty's steps began to lag. He had no idea how long it was since he had left the Ford home; it might have been a couple of hours or it might have been four or five. He had not thought to look at a clock when he started out, or on the way back. What was he going to say?

Whatever happened, he couldn't tell the truth because that would lead to more questions, dangerous questions, and somehow he didn't feel like telling a lot of untruths to people like the Fords. But he would have to be mighty careful after his experience of Shelagh's sharpness in picking things up. A few moments' reflection, however, showed him an easy way out. He would merely say that Uncle Hank wasn't in, and that he had walked about and lost his way. That was partly true, anyhow, because he really had lost himself until he came out so luckily by the Bull's Head.

Having settled what he would say, Dusty turned down Beverley Road and was soon knocking at the door of No. 49, and there, as if he had not had enough surprises for one day, he got another, but of a different sort.

Mrs. Ford let him in and, instead of asking where he had been, she merely said she was glad he had come back because she was just getting the supper ready, and was he hungry? Dusty said he was, which was as true as anything could be, and concluded that Shelagh and David must have given some acceptable explanation of his absence. Then he heard voices upstairs and went up. Shelagh and David hardly looked at him. They were in the middle of an argument because David had lost his best boat in the canal and they were trying to make out whose fault it was. They didn't even ask him if he had seen Uncle Hank. It was the same over supper. Captain Ford was bothered about some trouble with the ship's engines. The atmosphere wasn't unfriendly, it was just quiet, and somehow it gave Dusty a feeling of security he had never known before, and his anxieties seemed to be smoothed away.

Round about eight o'clock Mrs. Ford said it was time the three young people went to bed, and by now Dusty was so drowsy that he was only too ready to follow her upstairs. He had a wonderful hot bath, and then, wearing a fresh pair of David's pyjamas, he got into a bed which smelled of lavender and which was so soft it was like floating on a cloud. Mrs. Ford tucked him in and kissed him good night, just the same as she did Shelagh and David. He wanted to say thank you, only a lump came up in his throat and he couldn't say a word, but from the look on Mrs. Ford's face before she switched off the light, he thought she understood.

As he lay in the darkness, after David had fallen asleep, Dusty thought of the funny way things worked out. When you got all prepared for something, it didn't happen, and when you weren't ready, things happened all over the place. His thoughts roved over the strange events of the day, and particularly the last part at the hostel. That old cat came into his mind. He would never have dreamed there was a hole in the wall if it hadn't been for that old cat. As he dropped off to sleep, Dusty vowed that he would bless that old black cat as long as he lived.

CHAPTER IV

Nearly Caught !

A fresh wind was blowing in from the south-east next morning and, the tide being nearly at its height, the river appeared very full of water and very busy with craft of all kinds. Long strings of timber barges progressed smoothly up-stream, drawn by efficient little tugs. Coal lighters nosed their way to and fro, serving the small steamers anchored alongside, and the manifold business of London's river proceeded to the accompaniment of warning steam whistles and hooters and the peevish cries of the many gulls which hovered and swooped overhead.

The gangways of the *Tilbury Pride* sloped steeply up from the dock-side for, in addition to being raised on the tide, she was also nearly empty of cargo. A gang of stevedores had been working all night to clear her, but now there was a lull, and Bob Pepper, the cook, stood in the sunshine at the door of his galley dispensing mugs of tea to a couple of early callers.

Bob was an inveterate talker; his tongue was never still. He was also extremely inquisitive because, if you are a talker, it follows of necessity that you must have some listeners, otherwise your state of mind is apt to be misinterpreted; and if you are to be able to hold the attention of your listeners, you must have something of interest to tell them. Quite early in life, Bob had learnt that what people most like to hear is something, preferably of a derogatory or scandalous nature, about somebody known to them; and so, whenever he encountered

(c 392)

any person whose conduct seemed to him to be unusual, he started to probe for the reason.

Following this well-tried routine, Bob threw out a line; not, it must be said, with any great hope of a successful outcome, for one of his visitors was Tub Timkins, who had a notable reputation for minding his own business, and the other was Walrus, whose mutilations of the English language made him quite incomprehensible to Bob.

" You two fellers look like as if you bin up all night," he remarked pointedly, running bright observant eyes over the unkempt and weary-looking figures confronting him. " Wasser matter? Couldn't you sleep in that lovely 'otel wot the Company provides?"

" You hear dat talk about lovely 'otel, Tub?" yawned Walrus derisively, as Tub made no reply.

" I ain't deaf," replied Tub, who was fully alive to Bob Pepper's designs. " Sea cooks are like parrots," he added acidly, " they talk too much." And, Bob Pepper having been silenced for a moment, he motioned Walrus away with him to a quiet spot by a deck-housing.

Sipping his scalding tea, Tub looked with lowering eyes down on to the wharf-side, where a foreman was mustering the loading gang ready to come aboard and start the day's work. The truth was that Bob Pepper's remark had been more accurate than he knew. Tub and Walrus had been hanging about the warehouse all night hoping, under cover of darkness, to get inside to that pump case. But they had not reckoned on a gang working all night. Furthermore, they had not reckoned on the unloading being supervised by a party of dock police. There had been a good deal of pilfering lately, and the police were taking no chances when the warehouses were open for night work.

Nearly Caught !

Brooding over the results of their vigil, Tub could find only one consolation. He had been able to ascertain that the pump case was stowed in the middle of the crowded warehouse, which meant that it wouldn't be moved until some of the other goods had been cleared. That would give them perhaps a couple of days.

But this consolation did nothing to relieve another matter which was troubling Tub's mind. He was still kicking himself for the way in which they had allowed Dusty to get out of the hostel, and his brain was tortured with uncertainty as to what the boy might do next.

After his talk with Dusty in the dormitory, he had been sure that the boy had not spoken, but anything might happen now. If he was a menace before, he had now become ten times more dangerous. For Tub knew that, should he drop one word that would start inquiries about the Bellamy jewels, it would lead to another and much more serious affair—the disappearance of Ginger Green.

It was a warm morning, but Tub shivered.

It was *imperative* to find some way of dealing with that boy!

He swirled his mug viciously and shot the remains of his tea along the deck.

" Come on, blockhead," he said, and Walrus, wiping tea from his dripping moustache with a hairy hand, yawned cavernously and followed him along the deck to the gangway.

The absence of Tub and Walrus from the hostel overnight had not escaped notice. Hank and Squeaky, returning late from a visit to Rotherhithe, had found the dormitory untenanted.

The visit had been Squeaky's idea. He could see that Hank was very worried about his nephew's future. The captain had taken Dusty home for the time being, it was true, but how was he to know how long that would last? On one thing Hank was determined, and this he told Squeaky repeatedly: whatever happened, the boy should not go back to Hull.

Squeaky racked his brains; he was sorry for old Hank, and at last he remembered that he had a maiden aunt who lived down at Rotherhithe. "I dunno, mind you," he said cautiously to Hank, "but p'raps she might take 'im in for a bit."

Hank seized hopefully on the suggestion and, stiffly attired in their best shore-going garments, they set off immediately after their midday meal. And this, of course, was the reason why they were not there when Dusty arrived a little later on.

Squeaky's recollections of his Aunt Beattie were mainly based on her timely habit of distributing pennies when he was a very small boy, and it was not until they were sitting in the train that it occurred to him that this was quite a long time ago. "It must be all of thirty years since I last seen 'er," he informed Hank, and it began to dawn on him that Aunt Beattie must be, to say the least, getting on.

Owing to Squeaky's vagueness about the address, it took them the best part of the afternoon to find the small and excessively neat villa inhabited by his aunt. It turned out, after all, that they had been wasting their time, because, while she might have considered a little girl, Squeaky's aunt, now a sharp-eyed old lady of seventy-three with a handsome grey moustache, glanced possessively round her overcrowded parlour and declared flatly that she couldn't possibly have any rough little boys breaking up her furniture, smashing her ornaments and wiping their muddy boots all over her carpets. She pressed upon them the misery of a genteel tea, however, and kissing the disgusted Squeaky with moist affection, allowed them to depart at about seven o'clock.

On the way to the station, Hank indulged in some biting observations on old maids in general and Squeaky's aunt in particular and, by mutual desire for more robust society, they stopped at a public house, where they fell in with some old chums of Squeaky's. The rest of the evening passed in a manner with which this story has no concern.

And now Squeaky was sitting on the edge of his bunk groping on the floor for his socks. "Them two ain't been in all night," he grunted, straightening himself and looking round the dormitory with a jaundiced eye.

"Let 'em stay out, the bloodthirsty 'orrors," growled Hank, as he pulled on his trousers.

Squeaky leaned towards him confidentially. "'Ere," he began. But whatever it was he was about to impart will never be known, for just then there was a loud hissing noise from the dayroom. "Crickey! That there patch I soddered on the kettle 'as come undone!" exclaimed Squeaky, "and all the water's runnin' out."

And he jumped up and scampered out, his shirt tails flying.

The time was now getting on for nine o'clock and the Fords were just finishing breakfast. Even in the school holidays, which were now in being, Mrs. Ford made it a rule to have breakfast at half-past eight sharp. Captain Ford was engaged with the morning paper and the children were enduring that trying interval which lies between finishing a meal and receiving the signal to leave the table. David wriggled in his chair.

"All right, children," smiled Mrs. Ford. "You may go."

The two boys rose and hurried out, and Shelagh, who

had half expected to be detained for the loathsome piano, dashed after them. Captain Ford folded the newspaper and rose.

" I've got to go to the docks and see how they're getting on with the engines," he announced. " What are you doing, dear?"

" It's one of my busy days in the house, I'm afraid," sighed Mrs. Ford.

" Well, don't forget we're going to the theatre to-night," her husband reminded her, and Mrs. Ford smiled. As if she would!

On his way to the door, the captain paused. " Why not give the kids a treat too," he suggested. " Let them go to the pictures this afternoon. On me," he added humorously.

" As a matter of fact, Jim," Mrs. Ford replied, " Shelagh rather wants to go to Madame Tussaud's, and that would be more of a treat for Dusty than the pictures. The bus ride would show him a bit of London too."

" All right; and you know where to send the bill," said her husband waggishly, as he went out.

Before starting to clear the breakfast, Mrs. Ford permitted herself to linger a moment before the mirror over the mantelpiece. She had bought a new dress to wear for the first time to-night, but as she gazed at her reflection she wondered whether, instead, she would wear the old blue thing which Jim always said was his favourite. It was not often she was able to go to the theatre with her husband and she wanted to make the most of the occasion. As she wavered between the new dress and the old, her thoughts were interrupted by the ringing of the telephone bell. She moved to a side table and picked up the receiver.

" Yes," she said, in answer to a masculine voice, " Yes, Mrs. Ford speaking. My husband is just going out;

shall I fetch him? . . . Oh, it's you, Miller!" She listened, then in reply said: " He's behaving splendidly and we are very pleased indeed with him. This afternoon the three children are going to Madame Tussaud's . . . yes, after lunch . . . they will leave here about two. . . . Yes, I'm sure he'll enjoy it. Would you like to speak to him? . . . Oh, very well, I'll just tell him you called. Goodbye."

Mrs. Ford replaced the receiver and hurried upstairs to tell Dusty his uncle had telephoned and to tell them all of the afternoon's treat.

At the same moment, in a dilapidated call-box on a street corner between the docks and the hostel, Tub Timkins also replaced a receiver. The idea had been a sudden one and the ruse had succeeded beyond all his expectations. Already his nimble mind was forming plans, and an ugly expression of triumph twisted his thin lips as he pushed his way out of the box.

Standing outside was Walrus, yawning noisily.

" If you want a sleep, let's get along to the hostel and have one," said Tub briskly. " At two o'clock we're going places."

" Vhat place you got in mind, Tub?" Walrus inquired defensively, as they walked along.

" Madame Tussaud's."

Walrus stopped. " Yaas, but Tub," he demurred, " dat's a kids' place. Vhy go to a kids' place?"

" Because the boy'll be there too," said Tub succinctly.

But Walrus was not satisfied. " Vhat can ve do in place like dat," he asked, sensibly enough, " vith peoples all about?"

Tub was terse and to the point. " Listen, mug," he said, " I know by what went on at the telephone that he hasn't said anything yet. But the perishing little fool might open his trap any minute. Then what? It fairly gives me the jumps."

"P'raps he von't talk," said Walrus, who was sleepy and wanted to have a few hours in his bunk.

"P'raps nothing," Tub rejected vigorously. "Get this in your big nut. We've got our foot on a ladder you never come down. That boy is the only being in the world who's likely to send us *up* that ladder. Get me?" Tub paused to allow his words to sink in. "We're desperate," he added, "and we've got to take chances. Yes, and we haven't to miss any, either. Savvy?"

"It don't seem we ever going to rest no more," grumbled Walrus, who only had room for one idea at a time. As Tub walked on he yawned once more and lumbered along in his wake.

. . . .

As soon as they were old enough to look after themselves, Mrs. Ford had made a point of encouraging David and Shelagh to go about London on their own. As a result, they had a wide and practical knowledge of places of interest and the means of reaching them, and Dusty thoroughly enjoyed with them the ride on the bus to Madame Tussaud's. They had front seats on top, and it was a lovely, sunny afternoon of high blue skies and gracious clouds.

"This is Waterloo Bridge we're coming to," said Shelagh, as the bus raced past the drab lodging-houses of Waterloo Road, eager for the wide clean curve ahead. "It's a new one."

"And over there is St. Paul's," said David, pointing away to the right where the dome of the cathedral rose in massive dignity above the grey roofs of the city. "In the distance you can see the Tower of London too."

Nearly Caught !

"I know," said Dusty. "I saw them both from the ship."

"That's right. You can't see the docks from here. They're round the bend of the river."

Dusty nodded.

"Look this way too, Dusty," said Shelagh. "That's Westminster. Those towers are the Houses of Parliament, and next to them is Big Ben."

As they trundled slowly along the Strand, Dusty gazed down wonderingly at the crowded pavements and the streams of scarlet buses, gaily-coloured commercial vans, taxis and cars alternately speeding and crawling on their way as the traffic lights stopped and released them. Whitehall, the Nelson Column, and the famous pigeons in Trafalgar Square were duly drawn to his attention; theatre-land was pointed out as they passed the top of Shaftesbury Avenue; but from there onwards his two guides became less informative, Tottenham Court Road and the Euston Road being notably short of interest except for those in search of furniture or motor cars.

"What *is* this Madame Tussaud's?" asked Dusty as they climbed off the bus at last and crossed the road. "I've never heard of it before."

"*Haven't* you?" said Shelagh, for whom the costumed effigies held an endless charm. "Well, it's an exhibition of life-size figures all made of wax."

"But who are they?"

"Oh, kings and queens and all sorts of famous people, some of them still alive," Shelagh rattled on, as David paid their entrance money and they pushed their way through the swing doors.

"Whatever do you mean?" said Dusty, startled.

Shelagh laughed. "Silly! I mean, they're models. What shall we do first?"

The Bellamy Jewels

Dusty stood looking round him doubtfully. He wasn't at all sure he was going to like this exhibition. It sounded rather stuffy and somehow frightening, like looking at a lot of corpses. He would rather have stayed outdoors. The Zoo, which they had passed just now, would have been much more to his liking.

Facing the entrance was a wide flight of stone stairs with iron railings and brass handrails. The main stairs divided into flights ascending right and left, with notice-boards indicating Hall of Kings and Grand Hall respectively.

On the right of the entrance hall was an opening marked Hall of Mirrors, and in the corner at the back was a sinister-looking curtained doorway with an arrowed notice-board which said " To the Chamber of Horrors— 7d. extra ".

There were a lot of men and women and children coming and going up and down the stairs and into the Hall of Mirrors, but just then few of them seemed to be lured by the promise of having their blood curdled.

" Let's do the Horrors first, while there's not many people," said Shelagh, as Dusty seemed unable to make up his mind. " Come on. Have we got enough money, David?"

" Yes, I think so," said David, thrusting his hand into his trousers pocket and moving ahead.

" Wait a minute," called Dusty, still hesitating. " What sort of horrors are they?"

" Ooooo—they'll make your blood run cold!" said Shelagh, turning a ghoulish face over her shoulder.

Dusty looked past her to the darkened doorway. Suddenly two figures appeared in the opening. One was a lanky, clean-shaven fellow, thin-lipped and crafty-eyed, the other a seaman in peaked cap with a grimy sweat rag twisted round his neck, a great gorilla of a man with a sweeping blonde moustache.

"Crikey, my blood's running cold now!" cried Dusty. He turned and fled up the stairs, dodging frantically among the slow-moving crowds.

David and Shelagh, astonished, looked back at the doorway. Two rough-looking men were standing there, and they were undoubtedly watching Dusty's movements in a markedly unfriendly manner.

"Whoever can they be, David?" said Shelagh nervously.

"I don't know. Better catch him up and find out."

Dusty was waiting at the top of the stairs. Behind him was the entrance to the Grand Hall, which was in darkness except for the subdued light focused on the groups of wax figures ranged round the walls, each on its separate low platform roped off from the public. By the doorway stood a policeman on duty and visitors were passing to and fro.

Dusty's face was pale, but his first sharp terror had passed. After all, he'd told himself, there were lots of people about, and a policeman too.

"Who are those horrible men, Dusty," said Shelagh, rushing up to him, "and why are you running away from them?"

"They're after me."

"We can see that," said David impatiently, cocking an eye over the railings. "But why?"

"Because they want to—to——"

"They're coming upstairs now!" broke in David. "Come on. We'll go in here and mix with the people."

As the three children disappeared into the Grand Hall, Tub reached the landing and paused.

"You wait just inside the door where it's dark," he

instructed Walrus. " If that young demon comes out in a hurry you'll know he's given me the slip. Stop him and hold him till I come. Understand?"

Walrus nodded and took up his position. Tub tilted his hat over his eyes and stood for a moment peering into the gloom. Coming in from the daylight, it was difficult to see anything but the illuminated figures. He decided to work his way round the room in the direction followed by the sightseers. When his eyes became accustomed to the darkness he would soon catch up with the kids and, somehow or other, he would contrive to separate the three of them and seize the boy.

By this time the children had reached a group of wax-works entitled " Parliament—Past and Present ". Instinctively they had attached themselves to a small family consisting of mother and father and two children, a dark-haired boy of about the same size and age as Dusty, and a fat little girl named Beryl in a pink satin party frock with a huge pink bow on top of her head. Progress was slow because the boy, Freddie, continually lagged behind, and Father, who was short-sighted and determined to have his money's worth, insisted on identifying each character from the catalogue.

Shelagh and David kept close to Dusty.

" Have you seen those men come in here yet, Dusty?" whispered Shelagh.

" I thought I saw Tub over there just now," replied Dusty, looking round nervously, " but I haven't seen Walrus."

" Mum, can I 'ave an ice?" shrilled Beryl, tugging at her mother's arm.

" Ssssh! No. Look, there's Mr. Churchill."

" Well, can I 'ave a sanwidge, then?"

" No," said Mum crossly. " Be'ave yourself properly,

or not at all. Look, Dad. There's Lord Woolton. He's
the man for me."

" Ah," said Dad. " Quite a speakin' likeness."

"Mmmmm," said Mum dreamily. "Where's Freddie?"

Freddie, a chronic sufferer from adenoids, which partly
accounted for his sluggish disposition, was still lingering
before a select arrangement of British admirals and air
marshals, the particular object of his open-mouthed
admiration being the elegant figure of Rear-Admiral The
Viscount Mountbatten of Burma, his hero of the moment.

Freddie was a confirmed dawdler, and he was not at
first surprised when a hand seized him by the shoulder,
for his loitering habits had accustomed him to such treatment. But when the hand began to push him roughly
into an alcove with the Duke and Duchess of Windsor,
whom he had already dismissed from his mind as "soppy",
and a strange and sinister voice ordered him to keep his
trap shut, Freddie realized that this was something more
than the usual parental shove.

" Mum!" he bellowed. " Where are you? Muuuuum!"

Tub, the owner of the hand, sprang away from him
as though he had been stung, but Freddie continued to
roar, and a crowd quickly collected, hemming them both
into the alcove. Mum and Dad, with answering cries,
rushed to the rescue. David, Shelagh and Dusty found
themselves suddenly alone.

" Quick!" said David. " Now's our chance to get
away."

Walrus saw them coming. He moved out of the
shadows uncertainly and stood across the doorway. He
had heard the disturbance at the far end of the hall. He
was also uncomfortably aware that there was a policeman
outside on the landing. Indeed, the policeman had
seemed to be regarding him fixedly for some time.

" Let us pass, please," said David, politely but firmly.

" Vhat's de hurry ?" said Walrus, grinning alarmingly.
" You stay and talk vid me, den I buy you some chocolate,
yaas ?"

" We don't want your chocolate," said Shelagh stoutly.
" If you don't get out of the way, we'll call a policeman."

" Hey, officer !" called David.

Walrus stepped aside hurriedly.

When Tub arrived some moments later, having with
difficulty convinced Mum and Dad that he had mistaken
Freddie for a nephew of his, the children had vanished.

" Where's that kid ?" demanded Tub sharply.

" Gone," said Walrus gloomily. " Dey all gone."

" Gone ?" echoed Tub furiously. " D'you mean to tell
me you let 'em get away ?"

" Sssssh !" said Walrus, raising a huge admonitory
finger. " Policeman outside."

Tub swore. " You *fool* !" he groaned, leading the way
out and marching up to the uniformed figure. " If this
is your policeman," he went on, seizing the spiked helmet
and cramming it down on to Walrus's head, " he's a
dummy. Like you."

CHAPTER V

The Silent Three in Action

When the children reached home, Captain and Mrs.
Ford were about to leave for the theatre.

" I've put your suppers all ready in the dining-room,"
said Mrs. Ford. " Sardines and tomatoes and a jelly

trifle. We'll be back as soon as we can. Mind you're all in bed and asleep. And see that the back door's locked."

" Yes, Mummy," promised Shelagh soberly, and indeed, as soon as they had gone she went to assure herself that the door was already secured.

" You don't think those men will follow us here, do you, Dusty?" she asked, a trifle nervously.

" Of *course* not," replied Dusty, though he felt by no means certain. " They wouldn't *dare* come to the captain's house."

" They'd better not," chimed in David.

" That's all right, then," said Shelagh, her mind at rest. " Let's have supper. I'm hungry."

The time went by very quickly, for Shelagh insisted that they must clear away and wash-up as a nice surprise for Mummy, and it was past their usual bed-time when she and David found themselves alone together in the playroom.

" I think Dusty's nice, don't you?" remarked Shelagh, tidying away some books they had been looking at.

" Not bad," said David off-handedly. It was true that their visitor had behaved jolly decently over the chronometer while he himself had not shown up very well, but he had made his peace on that score, and he felt that, in return, Dusty might have given them a better explanation of the happenings at Madame Tussaud's. After all, he had ruined their outing.

" I think we should have him in the Silent Two," pursued Shelagh.

" But the Silent Two is *our* secret," objected David. " I don't like letting other people know about it."

Shelagh was not to be put off. " Dusty's *not* other people," she argued. " He's one of us now."

The Bellamy Jewels

David considered. " All right," he said at last, rather ungraciously. " But I must still be the leader."

" Of course," Shelagh assured him. " Listen. Here he comes."

Dusty looked concerned. " I say," he said, " it's half-past nine. Shouldn't we be in bed?" Mrs. Huggins had been very strict about bedtime, and the results of disobedience had been uncommonly disagreeable.

" Yes. Mummy'll be back from the theatre any minute," said Shelagh. " But first we've got something to tell you." She turned generously to her brother. " You tell him, David."

" We're the Silent Two, and we're going to make you a member," announced David grandly.

Dusty looked from one to the other. What on earth were they talking about? " But—what do we do?"

" We'll tell you afterwards. We've got to hurry before Mother and Dad get back. Just do everything we do."

David and Shelagh made circles with their thumbs and first fingers, held them to their eyes and peered fiercely at him. Then they cupped their hands behind their ears as though listening intently. Next, they clapped their right hands over their mouths, and finally they drew the first fingers of their right hands across their throats with a flourish and a blood-curdling gurgle.

Dusty was mystified by this pantomime, but he followed their actions faithfully.

David then said solemnly: " Say this after me: ' I swear my solemn oath not to tell a soul and to follow my leader.' "

Dusty repeated: " I swear my solemn oath not to tell a soul and to follow my leader."

" Give me your hand," requested David, holding out his own right hand.

The Silent Three in Action

Wondering, Dusty did as he was asked.

"Accepted by the rules of the Silent Three," pronounced David gravely.

"David's the leader and we do whatever he says," explained Shelagh. "But, of course," she added, with a warning look at her brother, "we can have an *argument*."

"Up to a *point*," allowed David.

Dusty listened to this exchange with a faint feeling of boredom. It was all very mysterious, but where did he come in? "Yes, but what do we do?"

"We *pretend*," said Shelagh eagerly. "You know— that we know somebody is up to something—or where something is. Then we keep very silent and David leads us on the adventure."

Dusty thought this over for a moment, the other two eyeing him expectantly. It sounded rather vague and dull. If only they knew what had happened to *him* since he crept on board the *Tilbury Pride*, it would make them sit up a bit. "Gosh!" he thought suddenly. His eyes darkened with excitement, for a startling idea had shot into his mind and, as it established itself, others came so fast that he could scarcely keep them in order. With a tremendous effort he calmed himself and tried to reason things out before he spoke.

The idea concerned Uncle Hank. First of all, why was Uncle Hank in a jam? Because if those jewels were found in the pump case and the police were called in, everybody in the *Tilbury Pride* would be questioned, and Tub and Walrus would say that Hank put them there and that he had smuggled them aboard.

Of course, Tub and Walrus might yet manage to get the jewels themselves, in which event anybody who didn't know them might think that Uncle Hank would be clear, but by this time Dusty had seen and heard enough to know beyond all doubt that Uncle Hank would never be clear so long as they and the jewels were at large.

But supposing—and this was the wonderful idea—supposing, under the vows of the Silent Three Society, he could persuade David and Shelagh to help *him* to get the jewels? Then there wouldn't be anything for *anybody* to find out. What they were all going to do with the jewels when they had got them was something that Dusty didn't consider at that moment.

All this had taken only a few seconds to pass through Dusty's mind, but it was long enough to make Shelagh and David's expectancy turn to something more intent. They seemed to sense the excitement raging inside him.

" I know a first-rate adventure," Dusty blurted out, " if you two will help me."

" What sort of adventure?" asked David guardedly, for he thought he saw signs of things being taken out of his hands.

" Let Dusty tell us what it is, David," chided Shelagh, with sisterly insight. " We can all have ideas, even if you are the leader."

Dusty fixed his shining eyes on Shelagh.

" I know where there's a bundle of diamonds and gold hidden away—enough to fill a—a—saucepan," he gulped incongruously.

David sniffed. A saucepan full of diamonds and gold! It sounded so extravagant that it didn't occur to him that it could possibly be true.

" That's the sort of thing we pretend all the time," he observed in a dampening voice.

" But this isn't pretending!" cried Dusty. " It's real. It's true!"

" D'you mean to say——?" David jerked upright and could only stare, and Shelagh's mouth remained open as she stared. Dusty was rather impressed by the sensation he had caused. He went on to improve the occasion. " There are rubies and emeralds and things as well," he declared, " and spanking big diamonds that would knock your eye out to look at them."

" And do you mean to tell us this is true?" breathed Shelagh.

Dusty nodded vigorously and David pulled himself together. It occurred to him that he was not behaving as much like a leader as was becoming.

" Where are these things?" he asked, trying to speak in a business-like voice.

" Hidden in a case in the warehouse," replied Dusty eagerly.

" Which warehouse?"

" The one where they put the *Tilbury Pride's* cargo."

" And you are certain they are there?"

" I saw them put there with my own eyes," Dusty asserted, and as he spoke he saw himself crouching in the fog on the deck of the ship, watching Uncle Hank stowing the bundle away.

David began to feel he was now taking his rightful place, and that he was carrying out his functions as leader with no little capability.

" Did you mark the case?" he went on.

" It didn't want marking. Anybody would know it in a jiffy if they'd seen it once."

Shelagh's mind had been pursuing the more vital and personal angle on this astounding story. " But who do the jewels belong to, Dusty?" she put in.

For an instant Dusty checked; then he came out boldly:

" My Uncle Hank was minding them for somebody," he said.

The Bellamy Jewels

"And did your Uncle Hank put them *in* this case?" David interrupted importantly, before Shelagh could say anything further.

"Only because he was minding them for somebody," repeated Dusty.

"Who?" said Shelagh quickly.

This was a poser. Dusty needed time to think out the answer. "I'm not sure," he hedged, and he saw a light of triumph leap into Shelagh's eyes.

"So your Uncle Hank *did* have some jewels after all," she cried jubilantly, her mind harking back to that earlier scene. But David's action was swift.

"That was before Dusty was in the Silent Two," he said decisively, "so it doesn't count."

Dusty thought, with relief, that this Silent Society was remarkably convenient, when it came to the point. But the truth was that David was beginning to feel more like a leader than ever before, and it was a very pleasing sensation. He determined to keep control of the situation. All the same, it was odd that a man who was minding a lot of valuable jewels should stuff them into a case which might be moved at any moment without his knowledge.

"What would your Uncle Hank say if we got these jewels and minded them *for* him?" he said thoughtfully.

"He wouldn't know, and I wouldn't want him to know," Dusty replied passionately. "It would be the best thing that ever happened."

Shelagh would have liked to ask a few questions regarding this baffling statement, but David saw what was coming and motioned her to silence because he was beginning to put two and two together himself. Suddenly he shot a keen glance at Dusty. "Is all this something to do with those tough tykes who were after you in Madame Tussaud's?"

The Silent Three in Action

Dusty swallowed uncomfortably as he assented, for this looked like being awkward. But in a moment he was able to breathe more freely, for it appeared that David was keeping his mind severely on the main objective.

"Does that mean they know the jewels are there too?" he asked, and Dusty nodded.

"Then we've got to work fast," decided David promptly. "We must get those jewels this very night. Golly!" he exclaimed, smashing his right fist into the hollow of his left hand, "this is something like an adventure."

Shelagh had begun to look rather thoughtful. "D'you mean we're going to the warehouse in the middle of the night?" she asked, rather uncertainly.

"You bet," David told her positively. "I've got it all worked out and all you have to do is follow me."

"And we never tell a soul," Dusty slipped in, as a reminder.

"Of course not."

It did occur to Dusty that, like himself, nobody had thought of what they were going to do with the jewels when they got them. But even if he had been going to raise the point, which was doubtful, there was no time then.

"Listen!" cried Shelagh suddenly. A taxi drew up outside and the door slammed. She ran to the window and looked out. "It's Mummy and Daddy. They're coming in now!"

"Into bed—quick!" ordered David.

Shelagh ran to the inner door and disappeared. David and Dusty threw off their jackets and shirts, struggled into pyjama jackets and dived into their beds, pulling the bedclothes right up to their chins. In a few seconds all was peace and quiet.

The Bellamy Jewels

Presently there was a faint creaking as Captain and Mrs. Ford stole upstairs. They paused outside the door.

"Shall we just have a peep at them?" they heard Mrs. Ford say in a low voice.

"Quietly, then," said the captain softly.

Footsteps tiptoed into the room. The boys kept as still as mice, trying hard to breathe evenly and keep their eyelids from fluttering. They heard one pair of footsteps creep into Shelagh's room. David, in the bed nearer the door, felt his mother bending down to him. He turned over and grunted sleepily, his heart beating fast. Mrs. Ford straightened herself.

"You'd never believe they could be such little demons, would you?" she whispered as the captain rejoined her.

There was silence for a moment. Then the footsteps retreated, the light was switched off, and the door gently closed.

The boys lay still, letting their eyes get used to the ghostly light of the moon which streamed in at the side window. When all was quiet David sat up. Dusty followed suit and they both got cautiously out of bed.

"Better not put on the light," whispered David as they groped for their daytime jackets. "They might hear the switch clicking." He went to the mantelpiece and picked up a torch, which he stuffed into his pocket.

Watching him, Dusty said practically: "We shall need something to open the case with. I've only got a small penknife and a pea-shooter."

David went to his cupboard and got out a screwdriver which he put in his other pocket. Then, as Shelagh appeared ready dressed in the doorway, he said importantly: "The Silent Three are going into action. You know the rules?"

The Silent Three in Action

They went through the silent pantomime with their hands.

" You know what to do?"

Dusty said: " Yes. Follow you." Shelagh nodded.

" Right," said David. " Let's go."

He turned to the side window and carefully pushed up the lower sash. Immediately below was the projecting roof of the scullery. Resting against the gutter on one side was a ladder left behind by a man who had been replacing some broken slates. David climbed out, sat down on the peak of the roof and lowered himself gradually till his feet came in contact with the ladder. In a few moments he was on the ground with the others beside him.

. . . .

The warehouse of the Ixion Steamship Company was in the middle of a line of vast barn-like buildings stretching for a mile or more alongside the Thames. Access to the river, where loading and unloading of cargoes took place, could only be gained through the warehouses themselves, or by means of the large double gates which divided the buildings one from another and by which lorries and vans went in and out.

At night all these gates were closed and bolted.

The main double doors in the centre of the Ixion warehouse building were also closed, but in one of them there was cut a smaller door about a foot from the ground and just large enough to admit one person at a time.

Immediately inside on the left was a small wooden sentry-box affair where the night watchman sat when he was not doing a round of the building, and where he ate his solitary meals and brooded over his selections for the football pools.

Facing the entrance was a flight of stone stairs leading

to the upper floors. On the wall above the staircase was an electric clock.

The night watchman, whose name was Alf Tucker, was a sober and conscientious little man, an ex-sailor. He lived in a turning almost opposite the warehouse, in one of a long row of small red-brick houses with front doors opening straight off the street into the parlour. On this particular night his wife Ivy had promised to bring over to him a nice packet of hot fried fish and chips at a quarter-past ten.

Promptly at this hour, Alf poked his head out of the small door and looked up and down the street. He could see quite a long way in the moonlight but there was not a soul in sight. It annoyed him to think that his wife could not arrive on time. He was a stickler for punctuality, was Alf. Indeed, he had to be, for once every hour, so that his boss Mr. Merryvale would know that he was carrying out his duties, he had to punch six time-clocks, each situated in a different part of the warehouse. His next tour was due to start at half-past ten.

Alf made clicking noises with his tongue against the roof of his mouth and swore softly. It was too bad. Now he'd have to leave his supper to grow cold. It took him half an hour to get round the building. He wondered whether he dared desert his post and nip home. It wouldn't take more than five minutes. He withdrew his head and looked at the clock. Five-and-twenty past. No, he couldn't risk it. He'd have to leave the door ajar so that Ivy could pop the fish inside and run home again to the children. It was strictly against the rules, of course, to leave the open door unattended, but she certainly wouldn't wait outside for half an hour, nor would she come over a second time. " Not if *I* know it," he could hear her say in her rather querulous voice.

Alf took one more look outside, picked up his torch, his bunch of keys, and his clock puncher and, leaving the door slightly ajar, set off on his round.

Across the way, in the front bedroom of Number 15 Tindall Street, Ivy Tucker, who knew her husband's time-table as well as he did, took up her screaming baby from its cot and decided that Alf would have to wait until eleven o'clock for his fish and chips.

Below, two boys and a girl ran stealthily past, crossed the road at the bottom and, keeping close against the wall, arrived at the half-open door of the warehouse of the Ixion Steamship Company.

A fresh wind was blowing off the river, stirring the refuse in the gutter. Eddies of dust and fragments of paper scraped along mournfully for a few yards and then sank as though exhausted. The door creaked on its hinges as it swung open a little wider. Shelagh shivered and turned up her coat collar.

Motioning to the others to keep behind him, David crept cautiously forward and peered into the doorway. A single electric light was burning in Alf Tucker's cubby-hole and another on the half landing of the stairs. There was nobody about and no sound. Beckoning, David stepped through the door and stood looking about.

"It'll be upstairs," whispered Dusty, joining him. "I saw the crane land the case on the first floor."

"Okay. Follow me."

David led the way up the stairs, Shelagh behind him, and Dusty in the rear. At the turn of the stairs they stopped and listened. The wind was whistling eerily through the upper floor, but there was no other sound except the distant hooting of the tug-boats on the river.

At the top they stood motionless and dismayed.

"Great snakes!" exclaimed David, using an expression

he had recently adopted from a book, " how are we ever going to find that case?"

Before them, in roughly ordered rows, were ranged stack after stack of packing-cases, crates, barrels, sacks, and bundles of every imaginable size and shape. One or two lights were burning high overhead, but they seemed like distant stars in the enormous gloom. The children drew closer together, overcome by the size of the task before them.

" Well," said David at last, taking his torch from his pocket, " I suppose we'd better— What was that?" he broke off, startled by the sound of a slight thud, as of a small soft object falling. He flashed the beam of his torch round about. A large rat scampered into hiding. Shelagh let out a stifled scream.

"Hush!" cried David. "There's nothing to be afraid of."

" It's only an old rat," added Dusty calmly.

" *Only!*" echoed Shelagh in tones of muted horror.

" Come on," said David sturdily, " follow me."

He led them up the nearest main alley between towering piles of merchandise. They moved slowly and quietly. The two boys glanced to right and left, intent on their search. Shelagh followed fearfully. She was beginning to wish she was safe at home in bed. Presently Dusty touched David on the shoulder.

" I know what this case looks like," he said in a low voice. " Wouldn't it be better if I went in front?"

" Well—all right," agreed David reservedly. " Just this once."

Shelagh said nervously: " Do you think we ought to go any farther?"

David groaned. That was the worst of girls. They never could see a thing through. Still, she did look a bit scared.

" Wait outside if you like," he said leniently.

" What, by myself?" quavered Shelagh.

A sudden gust of wind swept through the building. The lights overhead swung to and fro, casting grotesque shadows. A loose sheet of iron roofing lifted and fell with a shattering clang. Shelagh, imagining she knew not what, dived frantically into a small space between a tower of tea chests and some sacks of grain. The two boys scrambled after her. Shelagh clutched Dusty's arm. He could feel her trembling.

" What was it, Shelagh?" he whispered.

" I d-d-don't know," said Shelagh faintly. " I thought I saw something move, and then that awful noise . . ."

" It's nothing," said David valiantly. He squared his shoulders and stepped out into the alley. " Come on."

Dusty stood still, his head on one side.

" Listen!"

There was a distant sound of voices.

" It's only some people in the street," said David, after a pause.

" I thought I heard Uncle Hank's voice," said Dusty uncertainly.

" Well, *that's* nothing to worry about. Let's get weaving."

As the three children proceeded on their search, four more jewel hunters were arriving at the main door. Hank and Squeaky lagged behind, Walrus was fed up with the whole business, and Tub reckoned he'd been a fool to burden himself with a lot of amateurs.

" What d'you keep hopping about like a pea on a plate for?" he demanded, turning savagely on Squeaky.

" You made me take my squeaky boot off," whined Squeaky, " and I keep treading on stones."

" Vhy don't ve leafe de mugs 'ere and do de yob ourselves, Tub?" suggested Walrus, with a nasty look at Hank.

Tub hesitated. His plan had been to send Hank and Squeaky inside while he and Walrus kept Alf Tucker quiet—by force if need be. But the door was open and Alf Tucker was nowhere to be seen. He might be in the building or he might not. Tub made up his mind.

"You two wait here," he said, ". and when Tucker comes, keep him talking, see?"

"Suits me," said Hank carelessly.

Tub and Walrus climbed through the narrow door and disappeared. Hank and Squeaky looked at one another.

"Put your boot on, Squeaky," said Hank, with a gleam in his eye. "We're goin' to beat it."

By this time the Silent Three had branched off the main alley on which they started, and were exploring a turning to the right. Shelagh was now easier in her mind and was taking an active part in the search.

"What's the case look like?" she asked Dusty.

"Well, it's a huge square wooden thing with a kind of a hump at——" He broke off and pointed ahead excitedly. "There it is!"

They hurried forward, Dusty in the lead.

"Yes, this is it," he went on triumphantly. "Here's the place where it was opened. Give me the screw-driver, David."

David produced the tool and Dusty set to work while the others kept watch. The metal binding was coming away without much difficulty when David whispered sharply: "Look out! There's somebody coming. This way—quick!"

They ran on a few yards and darted round the corner of another alley to the left. It was very dark and narrow and smelt of cheese. Scarcely daring to breathe, they huddled together and listened. The sound of footsteps came stealthily nearer and nearer. Then it stopped. There was a muttered exclamation.

Dusty put his mouth to David's ear and whispered: " I'm going to have a look round the corner to see who it is. It might be Uncle Hank."

Slowly, with infinite care, he retraced his steps and cocked one eye round the corner. It was not Uncle Hank. It was Tub and Walrus.

Dusty stiffened with alarm. They had found the case. Tub was already at work on the metal strip. Dusty watched in helpless despair. Wasn't there anything he could do?

Suddenly he thought of his pea-shooter. Quick as thought he whipped it out of his pocket and inserted a pea. Walrus's back was towards him, his fat neck bulging over his muffler.

Dusty took aim and blew with all his might.

At that moment Alf Tucker, with one more clock to punch and his mouth watering for his fish and chips, pushed open a door at the far end. He had scarcely crossed the threshold when a bellow of rage and pain echoed through the building.

Alf was a stout-hearted little man, but there was no denying that he was startled. He looked round hastily for a weapon. A handy crowbar lay on a nearby packing-case. Seizing it, Alf pelted off in the direction from which the sound seemed to have come. As he ran, disturbing thoughts began to flit through his mind. Wild animals at large? Rubbish. He had left the door open; somebody had got in. He dashed round a corner. A huge fist shot out and struck him on the side of the jaw. In the brief instant before he fell, Alf's mind registered a familiar face. He hit the floor with a thud and lay still.

Dusty watched, aghast. His momentary triumph with

the pea-shooter had had terrifying results; terrifying to him, that is, but apparently of little concern to Tub and Walrus. For Tub, with an indifferent glance at Alf's crumpled figure, had turned swiftly back to the case, and Walrus was rubbing the back of his neck and complaining about man-eating bugs from foreign parts.

All at once Dusty became aware that a noise outside had been gradually increasing; it was the sound of a heavy motor vehicle bumping over cobble-stones. It seemed to come from the water-front. Walrus had heard it too.

"Somebody coming," he said apprehensively.

Tub listened and swore angrily. There was a screeching of brakes and then silence. Motioning to Walrus to follow, Tub led the way back to the main alley and turned right. Dusty realized that they were going away from the staircase and towards the crane delivery opening on the water-front. He beckoned urgently to David and Shelagh.

"It's those two men, Tub and Walrus," he told them in an excited whisper. "I don't know who that other man is, but they've laid him out."

"Where are they?" said David.

"Gone the other way to see what that noise was. If we're jolly quick we might be able to get the jewels and beat it."

The two boys ran to the case and Dusty set to work. Shelagh crept over to the prostrate Alf. She bent down and touched him gently, but he did not move. He was breathing, however, and a little colour had come back into his face. She fancied she saw his eyelids flutter. Shelagh looked round for something to put under his head. A few yards away lay a cloth cap. She straightened herself and moved to get it. As she did so a huge form loomed up at the end of the alley.

"Hey, Tub!" it shouted.

The Silent Three in Action

"David!" screamed Shelagh, pointing wildly.

The two boys grabbed her by the arm and ran.

"Dat kid—and the other two," growled Walrus, as Tub hurried up to him.

"Well, what are you waiting for? Which way did they go?" He gave Walrus a mighty shove. "I might have known that kid'd be up to something," he muttered as they ran. "I'll skin 'im alive when I catch 'im."

Alf Tucker slowly opened his eyes. Where was he? What had happened? He could hear running feet, some light, some heavy. Painfully he rolled over on to his side. His head was swimming and he felt very sick. He lay still a moment and tried to focus his eyes on an object on the floor beside him. A crowbar. What was he doing with a crowbar? Abruptly it all came back to him. Somehow he must get himself moving and sound the alarm.

"The stairs!" cried David, turning instinctively down a right-hand alley. Dusty, nimbler than the others, darted ahead.

"It's blocked!" he called.

They swerved to the left, dodging frantically through a jungle of garden rollers and lawn mowers. Behind them the handles of the rollers swung madly to and fro in a nightmare dance. Tub and Walrus, belaboured on all sides, plunged after them.

At last they emerged into a small space ringed on all sides with bundles of garden brooms, heavy rustic tables and chairs, hampers of bulbs, bundles of spades, and unwieldy garden barrows. Rising above all was a mountain of bulging green sacks stencilled in black with the words "Hop Manure".

"Over the top!" yelled David, taking a running jump. In a few seconds they had gained the summit. Dusty looked back. Tub and Walrus were already on the way up. "Quick, David!" he cried, seizing hold of a sack. David took the other end. They swung it once between them and heaved it down the slope. It caught Walrus full in the stomach and sent him sprawling. "One more!" cried David exultantly, and another green avalanche went hurtling down. Tub dodged desperately, but the hop manure was soft and spongy. He lost his balance, teetered madly on his heels, and fell back with a crash into a garden barrow. The boys turned and bounded down the far side.

Shelagh, who had wasted no time, whispered: "There's an opening down here that looks as though it might lead back to the stairs."

She led them quickly to a narrow lane smelling strongly of spices. David entered first, then Shelagh. Dusty followed more slowly. The scent of cloves and cinnamon had given him an idea. In the dim light he peered at the cartons and boxes on either side. At last he found what he was seeking. He took out his penknife, split open a carton, and slipped his hand inside. When he withdrew it he was clasping a small cardboard cylinder with a blue label. He ran the blade of his knife quickly round the edge of the lid, and then hurried after the others.

By a series of zigzags and deviations they found themselves looking out on to a main alley once more. They paused. There was no sign of pursuit. Indeed, the silence was rather sinister. Cautiously David put his head out and looked right and left. He drew back and whispered: "We've got back to the alley where the case is—down there on the other side." He pointed to the left. "But that other man's gone. You have a look."

Dusty leaned forward. Sure enough, there was the pump case, with the strip of binding hanging loose. Alf Tucker had vanished.

The Silent Three in Action

" Shall we risk it?" he whispered.

David nodded and stepped out, pulling Shelagh after him. They crept along, keeping close to the side.

Suddenly a hand shot out.

" Got you!" snarled Tub, twisting David's arm behind him. David let out a yell and kicked blindly. Shelagh screamed and dodged away as Walrus charged out from behind Tub. Dusty leapt on to a barrel. Holding the little blue cylinder at shoulder height, he waited, tense and alert, until Walrus was within a yard of him. Then he deftly flicked it in the air.

A thick cloud of fine black and grey particles enveloped Walrus's head and shoulders. He stopped short, waving his arms helplessly before his face. His mouth fell open; tears poured from his eyes. He seemed to stiffen and then his whole body was convulsed as sneeze after sneeze shook him from head to foot.

Dusty jumped to the ground. " Duck your head, David!" he shouted. Again he flicked his wrist. Tub fell back with a howl of rage. David wrenched himself free.

And now a fearful clamour split the air. It was as though all the fire bells in London had been touched off under one roof. Alf Tucker had sounded the alarm.

The three children ran for dear life—away from Tub and Walrus, away from the hidden jewels, anywhere to escape this terrifying din.

At the far end of the building was a half-open door. It was, in fact, the door by which Alf Tucker had entered. Shelagh and David dashed through and found themselves at the head of an iron fire escape. Without pausing, they clattered down; it no longer mattered how much noise they made.

At the foot they paused for breath in a shadowed space between two warehouses. Double gates eight feet high,

without foothold, locked, barred and spiked along the
top, divided them from the street. A hundred yards
away the river flowed serenely past in the moonlight.
They could see the sturdy outline of the *Tilbury Pride*.
Her mooring lights glowed comfortingly and she looked
very home-like. Somebody was moving about on deck
with a hurricane lamp.

"Where's Dusty?" cried Shelagh, looking round fearfully.

David looked back up the stairs. "I'd better go and
see."

"No, don't," begged Shelagh. "He'll come in a
minute." She looked longingly towards the river.
"Couldn't we go to Daddy's ship?" she ventured.

David, who had momentarily entertained the idea himself, instantly discarded it.

"Don't be silly," he said scornfully. "They'd get on
to Daddy right away. And what should we tell him, I'd
like to know?"

Suddenly a door slammed and Dusty came flying down
the stairs.

"They're coming!" he yelled, taking the last three
steps at a bound. "Can we get out this way?"

"Only through the dock gates," said David, "and
there'll be a watchman there and probably a policeman
too."

"Well, let's try, anyway," said Dusty as they dashed
round the corner of the building.

Above the din of the alarm bell they could now hear
shouts from the *Tilbury Pride*. More lights were showing,
and a group of dark figures had gathered at the head of
the after gangway. A police whistle shrilled in the distance.
A motor bike came hurtling up the street outside, its
siren screaming.

The Silent Three in Action

The children halted, confused and uncertain. Shelagh drooped against the wall. She was tired and frightened. The two boys looked about them desperately. Just ahead was a large motor van with a covered top and coach-built driver's cabin.

David's face lit up. " Let's hide in that van till the excitement's died down. Hurry!"

He ran forward, caught the hanging rope and swung himself over the tailboard. Dusty bunked Shelagh up and vaulted after her.

The van was empty except for a folded tarpaulin sheet.

" We can cover ourselves with this," said Dusty, shaking it out and motioning to the others to crouch down.

" We shall get in an awful mess," objected Shelagh.

" Oh, don't fuss," said David, pulling her down beside him.

" Well, anyway," said Dusty, as he wriggled in alongside and pulled the tarpaulin over them, " we've shaken off Tub and Walrus."

" Ssssh!" hissed David, " there's somebody coming."

They cowered down. Footsteps ran past and stopped. The van shook slightly, doors slammed, the self-starter whined, and the engine sprang to life. Before the children could free themselves from their covering, there was a convulsive jerk and the van shot forward.

Hiding was one thing, but being carried off willy-nilly was something else. Clinging to the sides, they scrambled to the open end. Two men came hurrying from a doorway and began to run, shouting, in pursuit. One of them wore a peaked cap and looked like a lorry driver.

" Hi! Where are you going with my van?"

The van drew rapidly away, the children gazing out helplessly.

" Hi! Stop! Stop!"

The Bellamy Jewels

The shouts grew fainter; the men were left standing. Missing the watchman by inches, the van bull-dozed through the dock gates and away up the street. The children, bounced and hurled about on the floor, had a distant vision of a policeman picking himself up from the gutter, helmet awry.

In the back of the driver's cabin was a small oval window. It was while they were flashing past a brightly lighted cinema that Dusty caught a glimpse of the driver's face, grim and reckless.

"It's Tub driving," he gasped.

"Oh, I hope he didn't see us!" cried Shelagh.

"Of course—he—didn't," grunted Dusty as a swing of the van landed David's elbow in the pit of his stomach. "We were all covered up. Besides, they were too anxious to get away to bother about anything else. They haven't even got the jewels."

"How do you know?" asked Shelagh.

"What do you think I stayed behind for?" Dusty began to giggle. "Gosh, it was funny! If you could have seen those two sneezing their heads off!"

"That pepper was a wizard idea," grinned David.

A sudden lurch threw the three of them into a tangled heap. "If only they'd slow up for a moment," he panted, "we could jump off."

But it was horribly clear that, red, green or amber, the traffic lights were all one to Tub. The van thundered on to a chorus of motor horns and police whistles.

It was David who first saw the police car with its wand-like aerial. They watched its advance with a strange mixture of excitement and dismay.

Suddenly they lurched from a side turning into a wide shop-lined thoroughfare. Trams, buses and market carts were slowing up for the traffic lights.

The Silent Three in Action

In the driver's cabin, Walrus, his head thrust through the offside window, yelled: " Police, Tub! Stand on de gas!"

Muttering savagely, Tub set the van at a narrow opening between a bus and a lorry piled high with vegetables. There was a hideous scraping noise. Walrus jerked his head back with an oath.

" Dey're comin' up behind," he shouted.

" Never mind behind," snapped Tub, his eyes fixed grimly ahead. " Look what's in front!"

Ahead was a junction of four main roads. From left and right trams and buses were sliding forward. The lights changed from amber to red. The trams increased their speed. Tub's face hardened. He jammed his foot down on the accelerator. Walrus shut his eyes and shrank back into his corner. There was a wild outburst of tram bells, motor horns, and screaming brakes. The van swept through the converging traffic and dived in among the waiting vehicles on the far side.

Walrus opened his eyes with a shudder and glanced at Tub with something near to horror. Tub's leathery face had whitened but he drove on unhesitatingly, his eyes darting from side to side. Without warning, he swung down a dimly lit side street lined with tall plane trees.

" Look alive, man!" he snarled. " Are they coming?"

Walrus roused himself and hung out of the window.

" I t'ink dey gone past," he reported. " Take anudder turn."

Tub peered through the windscreen. He could not see very well and, now that the crisis was over, he was beginning to feel a bit shaky. There seemed to be a turning to the left. He swung the wheel over. The van turned. Almost instantly Tub realized his mistake. Desperately he crammed on the brakes. But it was too late. There was a deafening crash and a shattering of glass as several tons of timber and scaffolding rained down on the bonnet.

Inside the van, the three children, bruised and frightened, lay still.

"Are you all right, Shelagh?" whispered Dusty.

"I—I—think so," said Shelagh faintly, beginning to sit up.

"Keep still," warned David, "till we see what they're going to do. They may be hurt."

But even as he spoke the van began to rock, and there was a tinkling of falling glass as Walrus struggled to open the door. A few moments later the two men hurried out into the street and disappeared without a backward glance.

David and Dusty scrambled over the tailboard and helped Shelagh to the ground. They were a sorry-looking little group, dirty, tired and dishevelled. Shelagh pulled out a handkerchief and dabbed at her face and neck. Her blazer was covered in dust and she gazed down in horror at the stains on her pink cotton frock. The two boys, ignoring her exclamations, began to take stock of their surroundings.

"Look, Shelagh. That notice-board!" cried David.

Fixed to the wall of a shed was a board which read:

REYNOLDS & CO.

BUILDERS AND CONTRACTORS

Timber, sand, cement, &c.

Shelagh glanced at it miserably. All she could think of was the state of her clothes and what she was going to tell her mother.

"They must have gone round in circles, Dusty," explained David. "This yard is only a few minutes from our house."

"Gosh! What a bit of luck!"

Shelagh lifted her skirt and groaned at the sight of her petticoat.

"Oh, stop moaning, Shelagh. We've got to get home to bed before Mother calls us."

"How can I go to bed like this?" wailed Shelagh.

"I can hear some people coming," said Dusty in a low voice.

"We must hurry, then," said David. "On the other side of that fence there's a footpath which runs past the bottom of our garden. Come on, Shelagh."

Shelagh stuffed her handkerchief hurriedly away in the direction of her pocket. As the two boys bunked her up over the fence, a small square of blue cotton with the initial S in the corner fell unnoticed to the ground beside the wreck of the van.

CHAPTER VI

Dusty is Bluffed

Next morning, when Mrs. Ford returned from an early shopping expedition, the captain met her with the announcement that the children wanted to go down to the docks with him. Mrs. Ford looked at him dubiously.

"I think they'd be better having a quiet morning at home," she said. "They had a busy day yesterday, and I thought they all looked very tired at breakfast-time."

"You're getting old, Mary, that's your trouble," said

the captain, smiling at her affectionately. "Why, when I was their age . . ."

But what he would have done when he was their age Mrs. Ford never heard, though she could have made a very good guess, for at that moment there was a loud and determined ringing at the front-door bell.

"See who it is, dear," she said, making for the stairs. "I must get on. I haven't even made the beds yet."

Upstairs in the playroom, David and Dusty were getting ready to go out.

"I don't fancy the docks so much, after last night," said Dusty, standing on one leg and rubbing his other shoe on the back of his trousers.

"Why not? You aren't scared, are you?"

"Of course not," said Dusty indignantly. "But I don't see what we can do. We can't get into the warehouse again in daylight."

"No," agreed David, "but we can hang about and see if we can pick up any clues. The Silent Three *never* give up, you know."

"I say!" cried Shelagh, bursting in suddenly from the landing, "there's a policeman downstairs!"

"What does he want?" said David, exchanging a startled look with Dusty.

"I don't know," stammered Shelagh. "I was in the bathroom and I saw him come in. I nearly had a fit. D'you think they've found out about last night?"

"How should I know? Anyway, this is where we keep calm and let him do the talking."

"Oh dear!" cried Shelagh distractedly, "suppose we're all locked up?"

"Don't be such an ass," said David impatiently. "We haven't done anything. Let's go and listen over the balusters."

Dusty is Bluffed

On the front doorstep stood a large and genial-looking police officer holding out a crumpled blue handkerchief.

"We found it near a wrecked van in Reynolds's yard, sir," explained the constable, "and as your laundry mark's on it, the sergeant sent me round to make inquiries."

Shelagh thrust her hand into her blazer pocket, and her face went pale. "Oh—my handkerchief!" she gasped.

"I see," said Captain Ford, examining the handkerchief. "Looks like my daughter's—same initial—and if you say it bears our laundry mark, I suppose it must be hers."

"Yes, sir," said the constable, producing a notebook and pencil from his breast pocket and licking the point of the pencil.

"But as she was asleep here in bed last night," went on the captain soberly, "I hardly think she can have been concerned with the wrecking of vans in Reynolds's yard." He paused, and added with a smile: "She's only twelve years old, you know."

"Oh-ah!" said the constable, somewhat nonplussed. "Well, of course, sir, it may have been there some time. Things have a way of disappearing off clothes lines these days."

"Yes, indeed," said the captain pleasantly, beginning to close the door. "Thank you very much, officer."

"Sorry to have troubled you, sir. Good day, sir."

As the captain turned away from the door, the three children came slowly downstairs. Behind them, with an expression of extreme exasperation on her face, came Mrs. Ford, carrying a pink cotton frock.

"You'll have to be more careful with your laundry, young woman," said the captain jokingly, waving the handkerchief in the air. "See this? It was found in Reynolds's yard by the police. A bit dirty too."

"Dirty!" exclaimed Mrs. Ford. "Have you seen *this*?"

She held up the pink dress and turned it from side to side. "What on earth have you been up to, Shelagh?"

Shelagh hung her head. The two boys stood behind her with wooden faces. The captain, who was seldom involved in matters of this kind and was inclined to treat them lightly, looked on with an indulgent smile.

"Come now, Shelagh," pursued Mrs. Ford firmly. "How did it get into this state?"

"I fell down, Mummy," mumbled Shelagh, her face as pink as the unfortunate dress.

"You fell down," repeated Mrs. Ford satirically. "It looks to me as though you've been rolling about in tar. *You're* not going to any docks. You're going to stay at home and wash this. Perhaps that will teach you to take more care of your clothes."

"Oh, Mummy! Can't I do it when I come back?"

"Certainly not," said Mrs. Ford, thrusting the garment into her daughter's hands and turning to her husband. "You take the boys, Jim. And please don't stand there smiling when there's nothing to smile about," she added severely.

The captain's response to this rebuke was to wink at his wife very solemnly and pick up his cap from the hall chest.

"Come on, boys," he said, waving them towards the front door. "But mind, I shall have to leave you to amuse yourselves down there. I've got some business to attend to."

* * * * * * * *

Dusty is Bluffed

Over his desk in the offices of the Ixion Steamship Company, Mr. Merryvale sternly regarded two of his employees who had come to report the theft of a van.

" And you say you saw some children in the van?"

" Yes, sir," replied the driver, twisting his peaked cap nervously between his hands. " Looked like the captain's kids to me."

" What captain?"

" Captain Ford of the *Tilbury Pride*, sir."

" And the other was that stowaway, of that I'm sure," put in the driver's mate busily.

" Stowaway?" echoed Merryvale, turning a perplexed face to Stark, who was moving restlessly about the room.

" A nephew of one of the men, Hank Miller," responded Stark briefly. " Stowed away at Hull."

" But Ford told me nothing of this."

Stark shrugged his thin shoulders and added: " I think he's looking after the kid."

" H'm," murmured Merryvale, leaning back in his swivel chair and gazing abstractedly at the ceiling.

There was a moment's silence. The driver and his mate exchanged glances of relief. It seemed that Mr. Merryvale's interest had shifted elsewhere.

" That's all, you two," said Merryvale, sitting up with a jerk and speaking briskly. " In future keep a better watch on your vehicle. No doubt I shall hear from the police about it in due course. Don't let it happen again."

When the door had closed behind them, Merryvale turned to his assistant.

" What does all this mean, Stark?"

" Looks to me as though these kids know a great deal more than we do."

" And you say the police called at Ford's house this morning?"

The Bellamy Jewels

"Yes. As I came down their road on my way here, I saw a constable ringing the bell."

Merryvale rose from his desk and began to pace up and down, hands in pockets.

"Some queer happenings last night, one way and another," he mused. "Alf Tucker, the night watchman, was here just now. He swears it was Tub Timkins who broke into the warehouse. And now this driver fellow says he saw the Ford kids."

"It's my belief the jewels are somewhere in the warehouse and they either got them away, or tried to, last night," said Stark shrewdly.

"Who? Timkins or the kids?"

"Your guess is as good as mine."

"I wonder . . ." said Merryvale, rubbing his chin thoughtfully with a well-manicured hand. "Listen, Stark. I've got to have a talk with these kids right away."

"Be a bit risky, won't it?" suggested Stark. "After all, if Ford got to hear . . ."

"Perhaps you're right," admitted Merryvale. "Never mind the Ford kids. Get hold of the other—this stowaway. Maybe I can find out something from him."

.   .   .   .

When Tub and Walrus ran from the wrecked van, instinct kept them to the narrow streets and back alleys of a thickly-populated area where police cars were unlikely, and indeed unable, to penetrate. As soon as it seemed safe to assume that they had shaken off their pursuers, Tub drew Walrus into a disused air-raid shelter, where they both slept uneasily for a few hours.

Walrus's slumbers were undisturbed by thought of any kind, but in the intervals of dozing Tub was visited by a brilliant idea. He said nothing of this to Walrus, but when the siren of a nearby factory proclaimed that it was eight o'clock, he gave his companion a dig in the ribs and rose purposefully.

"Vhere ve goin' now?" yawned Walrus, lumbering slowly to his feet.

"To the hostel first," said Tub briefly. "Get a move on. There's no time to waste."

Nobody saw them leave the shelter and they made their way without untoward incident until they came to Chandler's Market, where stalls and barrows already lined the kerb and the pavements were beginning to fill with early shoppers. Here Tub found himself obliged to step to one side to avoid colliding with a man balancing a box of live eels on his head. While pausing for the man to pass he overheard a remark which gave him a clutch of fear in the pit of his stomach and set the final seal on his determination to carry out his plan.

The remark came from an elderly, bearded waterman who was leaning against a wall on which there was pasted a printed notice, and it was addressed to a woman in an apron with her hair in curlers, who was gazing at the notice with gruesome interest.

"I knew directly I pulled 'im out that 'e weren't no ordinary floater," said the ancient, puffing clouds of smoke from an old clay pipe. "'Is 'ead were bashed in, and it weren't done by no paddle nor screw."

"Pore feller," said the woman, her eyes wide with a horror she did not really feel.

For an instant Tub stood as though turned to stone. The words had an awful significance. He turned his back and affected to be absorbed in the activities of a Jewish gentleman who was arranging a display of saucepan cleaners, elastic and celluloid combs in a suitcase propped up in the gutter. Against his will he was impelled to wait and hear more.

" And 'ow do I know that, you asks me?" went on the aged waterman, now fully launched on a topic which always found a ready listener. " I know it on account of that floater's 'ead were stove in afore 'e got *in* the water."

" Well, I never! You don't say, Mr. Phelps," said the woman, goggle-eyed.

" When a floater's been *drownded*," asserted the old man, " 'e 'as a certain look, which I should know consideratin' the number as I've pulled out in me time. When they ain't drownded, they ain't got that certain look. You mark my words," he added, waving his pipe emphatically, " this red-'eaded feller were a goner when 'e were shoved in, as they'll very soon find out when they 'old the inquest."

This was enough for Tub. Keeping his face averted, he hurried off to join Walrus, who was looking back for him.

" They've found Ginger Green," he muttered, urging Walrus along.

" How you know dat, Tub?" said Walrus, his jaw dropping in consternation.

" There's a police notice up on the wall back there, and I heard an old busybody babbling about a red-headed floater he'd pulled out of the river."

.   .   .   .

Down at the crew hostel Hank and Squeaky sat once more at the long table. Hank had his kitbag open on the form beside him and was methodically laying out its contents. Opposite sat Squeaky, with his elbows on the table and his head supported on his hands.

After a long period of cogitation Squeaky said: " 'Ere, why can't we get another ship and clear off out of it while we're safe?"

" Because of Dusty Bates, that's why," replied Hank,

Dusty is Bluffed

looking suspiciously from his possessions to Squeaky and back again.

"But 'e's still at the skipper's 'ouse," Squeaky pointed out. "'E'll be looked after."

"And who by?" demanded Hank fiercely. "Tub and Walrus. A couple o' bloodthirsty crooks who'd think nothin' o' doin' 'im in because 'e knows about them perishin' jewels. Talk sense."

Squeaky sulkily resumed his slow process of thought, his long face buried in his hands. Hank gave him a sharp look and ostentatiously turned his bag upside down over the table. Nothing more than a few scraps of dirty paper and a shower of tobacco dust resulted.

Frowning with the effort of concentration, Squeaky offered another suggestion.

"Why shouldn't we take Dusty with us, p'raps as cabin boy?"

"That's what I'm thinkin' o' doin'," said Hank heavily. "That's why I'm goin' to the skipper's 'ouse to get Dusty away." He rose ominously and leaned across the table. "And that's why I'm lookin' for my new vest and pants." He reached across and ripped open Squeaky's jacket. "I *thought* so. You're wearin' 'em, you thievin' little weasel. Orf with 'em."

Squeaky jumped to his feet, upsetting the form with a crash. The two men began to dodge clumsily round the table.

Outside, Tub and Walrus cautiously descended the area steps.

"Have a look through the window and see who's there," said Tub, glancing warily over his shoulder. "We got to watch out for the cops now."

"Miller and Vatts," reported Walrus, with a disgusted snort. "Playin' about like a couple o' kids."

"Anybody else?"

"Can't see nobody else," said Walrus.

"Come on in, then," said Tub. "I need a wash and a shave and something to eat. Then we've got to get cracking."

As they entered, Squeaky, his jacket half off and his trousers slipping down his thighs, made a wild dive through the inner door to the washroom, with Hank blundering after him. The door swung to behind them.

"Vhy don't ve do something about them two mugs?" growled Walrus.

Tub swept Hank's gear into a heap and threw it into a corner.

"For a very good reason," he snapped. "I don't like the look in Miller's eye. I reckon he knows more than he's let on."

Walrus thought this over for a moment. He didn't get it. The news of the finding of Ginger Green's body had shaken him pretty badly. He was ready to see danger at every turn.

"And vhat about de kid? Suppose he starts talkin' to de captain?"

"He won't," said Tub, taking off his jacket and beginning to roll up his shirt-sleeves. "Not so long as he thinks his uncle's in danger."

Walrus shook his head uncertainly. "But it ain't only Miller's nephew," he persisted. "Dere's dem oder two kids as vell."

Tub glared. He knew all this as well as Walrus, and better. To hear it in so many words made him nervous. He crossed to the window and peered out. The door to the inner passage opened slightly as he said venomously over his shoulder, "I've got a plan to take care of all three of 'em. But first we'll see what Dago Frank's got to say about it."

As he turned back into the room, Squeaky returned from the washroom followed by Hank carrying a set of underclothes. For a moment Hank and Tub eyed each other in hostile silence. Then Tub signed to Walrus and the two of them disappeared into the back premises, closing the door behind them.

"Fierce as a couple o' maggots, ain't they?" remarked Squeaky nastily.

Hank grunted and stooped in the corner to gather up his belongings.

"They was talkin' about Dago Frank's," Squeaky continued chattily. "P'raps they're goin' to live there."

"Let 'em," said Hank shortly. "And if you're comin' along the road with me, 'urry up and make yerself decent. I'm goin' to phone Captain Ford and ask if I can go and see 'im about Dusty."

.   .   .   .

"I've got some office work to do," said Captain Ford as he and the two boys mounted the gangway of the *Tilbury Pride*. "You two boys can amuse yourselves for half an hour, can't you?"

"Yes, Daddy," said David. "Does it matter if we go ashore? Dusty might like to see some more of the docks."

"All right," agreed the captain, "but don't get into any mischief."

The two boys drifted to the rails. The loading of cargo was still in progress, and there was plenty to interest them. But Dusty was ill at ease. Too many unpleasant things had happened on board the *Tilbury Pride*. He looked about him apprehensively. He wished Uncle Hank would turn up.

"What are we going to do, David?" he said uncertainly.

David, whose brows were drawn in thought, said: "I'm trying to work out a way of getting to that case."

"We can't do much from here."

"I know. That's why I asked Daddy if we could go ashore."

"Well, let's go, then," said Dusty promptly.

"Don't rush me," said David. "You have to make jolly careful plans on a job like this. We can't take too many chances."

"Well, I've taken a few," said Dusty defensively. He glanced down the deck to the after gangway. "I say, who's that man staring at us—the one who's just come on board?"

"He's from Mr. Merryvale's office," said David, following his glance.

"Who's Mr. Merryvale?"

"He's the boss of the shipping agents."

As they spoke, the thin perky figure of Joe Stark advanced smilingly towards them.

"Hullo, David," he said, with assumed joviality. "Is this the stowaway?"

"Yes," replied David, smiling back.

Dusty said nothing. He was getting rather tired of being referred to as "the stowaway", as though he was some kind of freak.

"I've got a message for you, sonny," said Stark, running a seemingly kindly eye over him. "Mr. Merryvale would like to see you in his office."

"What for?" asked Dusty suspiciously.

"He's interested in you; he wants to help you."

Dusty, partly reassured, looked at David questioningly.

"You may as well go," responded David. "He's

Dusty is Bluffed

very important, is Mr. Merryvale. Perhaps it's good news."

" All right," said Dusty slowly.

" If I'm not here when you get back," David added meaningly, " go on home."

" Okay," said Dusty, turning to accompany the smiling Stark. But they had not gone very far before he began to have misgivings. It was true, of course, that David knew Mr. Merryvale, and this man Stark seemed a decent sort of egg, but grown-up people had an awful way of making you say things you didn't mean to say, and Dusty had a great deal to conceal. By the time they were mounting the stairs of the office building, he was ready to turn and run. But Stark had somehow contrived to be behind him, and as they reached the top a door opened and a tall, dark gentleman, elegantly dressed, stood smiling genially down at him.

" Ah yes. Come in, my boy," he said, moving aside and, with a slight inclination of the head, motioning Stark towards the inner office. " I'm Mr. Merryvale."

Dusty entered and looked round wonderingly. He had never been in such an office before. His attention was caught at once by a large model of a sailing ship in a glass case by the window.

Mr. Merryvale went to his desk and sat down.

" So you are the boy that stowed away in one of our ships," he remarked, his eyes beaming benevolently behind his horn-rimmed spectacles.

Dusty nodded, still slightly overawed by Merryvale's appearance and surroundings.

" What's your name?"

" Dusty Bates, sir."

" I believe you're Hank Miller's nephew?" pursued Merryvale in kindly tones.

"Yes, sir," said Dusty, more confidently. His eyes turned again to the model ship. Merryvale watched him indulgently.

"You like ships, do you, Dusty? Come over here and tell me about yourself."

Dusty came forward with a smile.

"Yes, sir. I love ships," he said, warming to Merryvale's friendliness.

"It sounds to me as if you want to be a sailor."

"Not a sailor, sir; a captain," protested Dusty. "Uncle Hank says sailoring's a dog's life," he added confidingly.

"Oh, he does, does he?" laughed Merryvale. His manner changed slightly as he went on quickly: "Then why did you follow him aboard the *Tilbury Pride*?"

"I wanted to get away, sir. I haven't any proper home. My mother and father are dead. I wanted to go to sea and earn my own living."

Dusty paused, feeling that perhaps he had said too much. But Mr. Merryvale continued to smile at him amiably.

"Well, we must see what we can do to help you. But, first, there is something I want you to do for me."

Dusty's face brightened. Mr. Merryvale leaned forward confidentially.

"Dusty, I want you to tell me about something that happened in the *Tilbury Pride*."

Dusty stepped back. Merryvale's eyes seemed to be boring into him. "I don't know what you mean," he said guardedly.

"Yes, you do," insisted Merryvale quietly. "What *did* happen, Dusty?"

"I don't know, sir," hedged Dusty uneasily; "I was asleep most of the time."

Dusty is Bluffed

Merryvale's expression hardened. There was a sharper note in his voice as he tried another approach.

"Dusty, why did the police call on Captain Ford this morning?"

Startled, but relieved to be able to reply truthfully, Dusty said: "Oh, that was only about Shelagh Ford's handkerchief. They laughed about it."

"But perhaps it wasn't so simple as all that," suggested Merryvale, with a hint of menace. "Perhaps the policeman had another idea."

Dusty gazed at him blankly. "What about, sir?"

"Dusty," said Merryvale gravely, "you like Captain Ford, don't you?"

"Rather, sir," said Dusty warmly.

"I happen to know he is in great danger."

"Captain *Ford*?" exclaimed Dusty, his eyes wide with astonishment.

"Yes, Dusty," said Merryvale in tones of deep concern. "In danger of being sent to prison, ruined and disgraced. I am very worried over what will happen to his family."

Dusty gazed at Merryvale in bewilderment, his mind a turmoil of doubt and alarm. He thought of Captain Ford, so kind and just, so very much his idea of what a sea captain should be. He could not believe it. "Captain Ford sent to *prison*?" he repeated.

"Over those jewels, Dusty," said Merryvale, pronouncing each word with deadly emphasis and watching his victim like a snake with a rabbit.

"The jewels in that crate?" burst out Dusty, shocked out of all caution and blind to the swift gleam in Merryvale's eyes.

"They are stolen jewels, Dusty. Poor Captain Ford is in the power of the criminals. That is why he stopped the police from finding them. Now he is in danger every minute, unless you will help me to recover the jewels and return them where they belong."

"Oh yes, sir, I will," said Dusty fervently. "I'll do anything to help Captain Ford."

"Right," said Merryvale briskly. "Now, where are the jewels, Dusty?"

Unhesitatingly Dusty replied: "In a big crate in the warehouse. It's shaped like this." He indicated the shape, size and height of the pump case. "It's still there, because we saw it last night."

"Who else knows where the jewels are?"

"Only Shelagh and David Ford, and Uncle Hank, and Tub and Walrus, I think," reeled off Dusty, unconscious of the consternation in Merryvale's face. "Oh, Mr. Merryvale, you will save Uncle Hank and Captain Ford, won't you?"

"Trust *me*, Dusty," said Merryvale, rising and leading the boy to the door. "And mind, not a word to the other children, or *anybody*. We're working together."

"You bet, Mr. Merryvale," said Dusty solemnly.

"Where are you going now?" inquired Merryvale casually, as he opened the door.

"Back to David," said Dusty. "But I shan't tell him how we're working together."

"I think that is very wise," said Merryvale gravely. "Good-bye, Dusty."

As Dusty clattered down the stairs, his mind agog with all he had learned, Merryvale turned to Stark, who had entered from the inner office.

"The Bellamy stuff is in a case in the warehouse," he announced, whipping off his glasses and mopping his face with an expensive silk handkerchief. "Phew! Those three kids know too much for us—*and* for those

Dusty is Bluffed

double-crossing rats. If Tub and Walrus get hold of them
—let them—they're ruin for all of us. But find Tub and
Walrus. Don't let them out of your sight. If they go
near the warehouse. let me know. Get busy."

. . . .

David was the first to reach home. He found his
mother in the dining-room, standing by the telephone
with an anxious look on her face.

"Have you seen Shelagh, David?"

"No, Mother."

"I can't think what has become of her. I left her
washing her frock in the kitchen, and when I went back
she wasn't there. That was two hours ago."

"I expect she's gone to see one of her friends," said
David vaguely.

"I've telephoned Mrs. Wills and Mrs. Graham and
they haven't seen her. Besides, she would have asked me.
I told her not to go out."

"I shouldn't worry, Mother," said David lightly.
"She'll turn up presently. Has Dusty come back?"

"No," said Mrs. Ford. "And that's another thing,"
she went on rather crossly. "His Uncle Hank keeps on
ringing up and asking for your father. I've done nothing
but answer the telephone all the morning. There it goes
again, you see." She picked up the receiver. "Yes,
this is Mrs. Ford. . . . No, he's not back yet. . . . No,
Dusty isn't here either. My son David has just come
home alone. You haven't seen my little girl anywhere, I
suppose? . . . I don't know where she can have got to.
She's been missing for over two hours and I'm getting
worried. . . . Yes, I wish you would, Uncle Hank. Good-
bye."

Mrs. Ford replaced the receiver with a sigh.

" He says he'll keep a look-out for her," she said to David. " I don't know what else I can do."

" She'll turn up," said David optimistically. " She always does, you know. Can I have something to eat?"

" There's some cake in the tin in the larder. You can have a slice of that," said Mrs. Ford, picking up a duster and setting to work with a worried frown. " The meal won't be ready yet."

David made his way to the kitchen. He was standing by the table with a knife poised over the cake tin when the back door opened, and Dusty came in holding a small piece of paper in one hand.

" Hullo! Have some cake?" said David, cutting two substantial slabs and handing one to Dusty.

" Thanks," said Dusty taking the cake in one hand and holding out the paper with the other. " I say, look at this. I can't make it out. It's from Shelagh."

David read the note, looked at the other side of it, and then at Dusty.

" Where'd you get it?" he said, puzzled.

" From a boy outside. He ran up to me just as I was coming in at the gate and asked if I lived here. When I said yes, he stuffed this into my hand and rushed off."

" How odd!" said David. " Mummy's rather worried about Shelagh. She hasn't been seen for a couple of hours." He looked at the note again. " Both come at once to the corner of Fortescue Road by the towpath," he read aloud. " Say nothing. Uncle Hank is here. Very important."

" What d'you make of it?" asked Dusty.

David took a large bite of cake. " Well, for one thing, it doesn't look much like her writing to me," he mumbled doubtfully.

"Who else could it be? Besides, she says Uncle Hank is there."

"That's funny!" exclaimed David. "He's just been talking to Mother on the telephone. She asked him if he'd seen Shelagh, but he said he hadn't. So she *can't* be with Uncle Hank."

"Gosh! we'd better do something about this. Where's Fortescue Road?"

"About ten minutes from here," said David, making for the back door. "Come on. We'll slip out this way quietly."

CHAPTER VII

Uncle Hank to the Rescue

Frank's Café was one of those shabby little double-fronted shops which are to be found by the dozen in the back streets of any big city. The paint had peeled from its woodwork in ugly blotches; the lower half of its windows had been painted black, and the curiosity of the passer-by was further discouraged by dingy lace curtains. In its early days it might have been a prosperous little grocery store, but it was many years now since the local inhabitants had known it as anything else but Frank's Café, a place of dubious reputation, avoided by respectable citizens and by all whose sole purpose in entering a café is to obtain wholesome food and drink.

As for the proprietor, if his name was not Frank, he had long since forgotten it, along with many other inconvenient details of his past. With a steaming tea urn on one side of him and a glass case of fly-blown sandwiches and buns on the other, Frank sat perpetually on a high stool behind his counter at the back of the shop, immobile as a toad, his heavy-lidded eyes observing everything, surprised at nothing. Behind him, on shelves which reached to the ceiling, was a varied collection of china cups and saucers and plates, and a few bottles of innocent-looking soft drinks. Frank had no licence to sell intoxicating liquor, but that is not to say that he could not provide it when it seemed likely to be to his advantage.

Alongside the counter, on one side, a narrow wooden staircase led to the upper floors.

On this particular noon-tide Frank sat, as usual, behind his counter, studying a newspaper spread out before him. He wore no collar, and his grimy shirt was open at the neck. His black hair fell in oily rings over his forehead and a trickle of sweat ran down the folds of his double chin on to his hairy chest. It was a warm day and, moreover, Frank still found some difficulty in reading an English newspaper. Breathing heavily, he traced the lines of print with a podgy forefinger on which there sparkled a handsome diamond ring.

There were only three customers in the shop. One of them, a rough-looking seaman, lay sprawled across a table, apparently asleep, a little cloud of flies buzzing lazily over his head. Standing by a pin-table against the wall were two flashily-dressed young men idly passing the time with a game. The snores of the seaman and the rattle of the balls in the pin-table were the only sounds to be heard.

Suddenly the narrow double doors burst open and two men blundered in from the street, each pushing before him a kicking, struggling youth.

Frank looked up from his newspaper, met the ques-

tioning eyes of Tub Timkins, and inclined his head
slightly towards the staircase. There was no change in
his expression, and almost at once he resumed his reading,
pausing only to direct a cautionary glare at the pin-table
players. A nod was as good as a wink to these worthies,
who discreetly turned their backs and went on with their
game.

The snores of the sleeping seaman ceased abruptly,
but only he was aware of that, for the youths were putting
up a vigorous fight, and their passage through the café
and up the stairs was accompanied by the crash of over-
turned chairs and an assortment of grunts, groans and
cries.

When all was quiet once more, the seaman, whose
name was Sam Leatherbottle, slowly reared himself up
from his table, stretched his arms, yawned realistically,
and, with a casual salute to Frank, ambled slowly out into
the street.

At the top of the house in a small L-shaped attic, lit only
by a skylight, David and Dusty, dishevelled and breathless,
gazed at each other with unconcealed panic as the key
turned in the door behind them. Neither of them heard the
soft sliding back of a small panel in the upper part of the
door, nor did they notice that there was no sound of
retreating footsteps, for from behind a rolled-up mattress
in a corner of the room appeared the towsled head and
tear-stained face of Shelagh.

"Shelagh!" exclaimed David. "How did *you* get
here?"

"Those awful men, Tub and Walrus, brought me
here in a car," gulped Shelagh, her tears beginning to
flow again from sheer relief at seeing the two boys.

"But how did it happen? Mummy said you weren't
to go out"

Shelagh stared at her brother. " Then that note wasn't from you?"

" What note? I didn't send you any note."

Shelagh sniffed back her tears and said shakily: ." While I was washing my frock in the kitchen, somebody pushed a note under the door. It was from you and it said to go to Fortescue Road at once—you know, by the old tow-path. So of course I went."

" Golly! They caught us the same way."

" Well, anyway, we've found Shelagh," said Dusty, trying to make the best of things. " And now we must try to get away. How about that skylight, David?"

The three children gazed up at the small square of glass. It would be quite easy to open it if only they could get up there. Spanning the walls just below it was a stout oak beam.

" You climb up on my back, David," said Dusty, bending over.

David judged the distance with his eyes and shook his head. " No, that won't do. Look, I'm taller and stronger than you." He bent down and braced his hands on his knees. " You have a go."

Aided by Shelagh, Dusty climbed on to David's back and reached up for the beam. He could barely touch it with his finger-tips. He scrambled down again.

" Oh dear!" cried Shelagh. " Whatever shall we do?"

" Why shouldn't we all shout and kick up a row?" suggested Dusty. " Somebody might hear."

" Oh no, don't do that," begged Shelagh. " I tried, and an awful-looking fat man came up and said he'd tie my head in a sack if I didn't shut up."

The Silent Three gazed at each other gloomily. Then David said to Dusty: " I say, I forgot to tell you. Those jewels aren't in the warehouse any more."

Uncle Hank to the Rescue

"What's the use of talking about that, David?" said Shelagh distractedly. "The important thing is to get out of here."

"All right. Keep calm," said David. "I was only going to tell him that I saw the big case taken away by lorry." He turned to Dusty, who stood open-mouthed with dismay. "I followed in a taxi. It's in the gas-works."

Dusty's thoughts flew back to his conversation with Mr. Merryvale, who had to have the jewels to save Captain Ford and Uncle Hank.

"Suppose they've opened it?" he said, horrified.

"They won't for two or three days. I heard a man say so. It's gone into a sort of stores."

"Who *cares* where it is!" cried Shelagh, stamping her foot angrily. "What's going to happen to us if we can't get away from this awful place?"

Outside on the landing, Tub Timkins, with a satisfied smirk, silently closed the small trap-door and crept downstairs. His plans had succeeded beyond his wildest hopes. For good measure the children had even revealed the whereabouts of the jewels. And in a short time now—so short that he did not even consider the possibility of their escape—they would be out of the way for ever.

It only remained for the tide to turn.

. . . .

Joe Stark was an astute young man, and when his boss Merryvale ordered him to find Tub and Walrus he knew at once that he would need some help. He could keep an eye on the warehouse himself and at the same time make some useful inquiries; but it seemed to him unlikely that Tub and Walrus would make, in daylight, any further attempt to enter the warehouse. Born and bred in dockland, nobody knew better than Joe the haunts of shore-going seamen, and he had a hunch that they would be lying low at Frank's Café.

It was while he was pondering this idea that Joe encountered Sam Leatherbottle strolling dejectedly along the wharf.

Sam was a good-natured chap and, so long as he had money to spend on beer and amusements, he had no particular leanings towards wrongdoing. Unfortunately Sam's good nature caused his money to disappear with remarkable speed as soon as he got ashore, and if you happened to catch him when his pockets were empty, he would readily listen to any reasonable proposal which might help to refill them. And so it came about that Sam took a cup of tea and a midday nap in Frank's Café.

Sam's report of events was prompt and accurate. He was well satisfied with two half-crowns and went off jingling them happily while Joe Stark hurried back to the London office of the Ixion Steamship Company.

"A bit of news, guv'nor," he said, breaking in on Merryvale without ceremony. "Sam Leatherbottle just told me he saw Tub and Walrus running those kids into Dago Frank's."

"Fine," said Merryvale, rubbing his hands together. "That means they're taken care of."

"But there's a bit of not so good news," went on Stark, who had used his own time to some purpose. "The crate's not in the warehouse."

Merryvale's air of complacency vanished. "Where is it?" he snapped.

"You can search me, guv'nor. There were a dozen crates off the *Tilbury Pride*. They've all been cleared."

"But you can trace it, man," said Merryvale impatiently. "I told you the shape. Ask the dispatch man."

Uncle Hank to the Rescue

"They go by labels, not shapes. But that kid must have seen a label or marking."

"Well, ask him."

Stark's face expressed the liveliest apprehension. "If I go to that café they'll cut me up, guv'nor!"

"Get hold of that boy by hook or by crook," said Merryvale ruthlessly. "Find out where the crate's gone and bring the stuff back here. Now, beat it."

$\bullet \quad \bullet \quad \bullet \quad \bullet \quad \bullet \quad \bullet \quad \bullet \quad \bullet$

Hank Miller was not renowned for his speed in putting two and two together; for that matter, neither was Squeaky. After his last telephone conversation with Mrs. Ford, some little time elasped before, in a flash of inspiration, it dawned on Hank that perhaps he and Squeaky had a clue to Shelagh's disappearance and Dusty's failure to reach home.

"'Ere, wot was that you was sayin' about them two crooks and Dago Frank's?" he said, turning on Squeaky with such violence that Squeaky flinched involuntarily.

From certain well-known signs in Hank's manner Squeaky saw trouble ahead. "They was talkin' about it," he said warily, keeping an eye on him.

"About what?" rapped Hank.

"About wot I told you," said Squeaky evasively.

By this time Hank's mind was working at top speed. He was sure he was on the right track. His excitement rose. Controlling himself with difficulty, he fixed Squeaky with eyes as hard as two boiled sweets.

"Can't you answer a straight question without a lot of 'ummin' and 'ar-in', or are you doin' it on purpose?" he demanded. "Come on. Out with it. Wot *was* they sayin'?"

Hank could hardly contain himself as he watched Squeaky scratching his head and searching his mind.

" I can't remember the exact words," he said at last.

Hank made an impotent gesture imploring help from some unspecified quarter.

" Never mind about exact words," he shouted. " What was it *about*?"

" All right, all right!" said Squeaky, with a sudden access of spirit. " There's no need to lose yer temper. It was somethin' about havin' an idea for all of 'em, and seein' wot Dago Frank had to say about it." He was going to add a defiant reminder that he had told Hank at least twice before, but he didn't have time.

" That's it!" exulted Hank, smacking his right fist into the hollow of his left hand. Then, lowering his voice to withering scorn: "And you didn't think it was important."

" More didn't you," Squeaky reminded him promptly and hopefully. But, as he told himself dolefully at once, you never knew quite what you were up to with Hank, for he retorted:

" I didn't 'ear it, did I?"

" Maybe not, but I told you," Squeaky persisted.

" 'Earing's one thing; being told's another," propounded Hank, and while Squeaky was trying to unravel this piece of tortured logic, he went on, verifying his own thoughts as much as speaking to Squeaky: " It's as clear as mud in yer eye. Them kids are in Dago Frank's and them crooks 'ave put 'em there. And wot's more," he asserted fiercely, " we're goin' to get the kids out of it."

Squeaky eyed him apprehensively.

" After Tub and Walrus 'ave gone, like," he amended quickly.

" Whether they've gone or whether they ain't," said Hank emphatically. " Come on."

Uncle Hank to the Rescue

Squeaky hung back. "Don't let's 'urry too much," he suggested. "There might be another way of doin' it without runnin' into them two."

"Ho, yes," scoffed Hank. "A bit more of your brain-work comin' into play. Why, if a man run 'alf a mile to 'it you on the 'ead with a big 'ammer in broad daylight, you wouldn't know wot 'e was up to till you woke up in 'ospital. And even then you'd 'ave to be told." He took Squeaky by the arm and dragged him along. "Come on, can't you?"

Squeaky gave in, but not without further expostulation. Fool'ardy, he reckoned it was, and he said so. But Hank was his buddy, so he tagged along. He was not going to take any unnecessary risks, however, and his first act on arriving at the café was to nip down the side passage while Hank had what he called a dekko through a rent in the lace curtains.

When he rejoined Squeaky, Hank's expression was grim and determined.

"There's Tub and Walrus and that there Dago all 'uddled together over the counter," he reported. "You can tell they're 'atchin' somethin'. Those kids are 'ere, I'll bet me life."

"But you ain't *sure*," said Squeaky cautiously.

"Oh yes, I am," said Hank, peering down the passage and up at the roof. "I shall 'ave to 'ave a look round from the top and that means you'll 'ave to make a bit of a set out down below."

"Such as wot?" inquired Squeaky, his worst fears beginning to take shape.

"Anything," said Hank airily. "A bit of a row'll do."

Squeaky was appalled. "A bit of a *row*? *Me*—with them two?"

"That's wot I said."

The Bellamy Jewels

" 'Ave you gorn *barmy*?" inquired Squeaky. " You might as well tell me to go into a tiger's cage and pull 'is whiskers."

" I don't mean start a *real* row," said Hank, beginning to lose patience. " Pretend to start one."

" But 'ow do we know *they'll* pretend?" objected Squeaky obstinately.

" Oh, fer cryin' out loud!" groaned Hank. " *Don't* start a row, then. Just walk in and talk to 'em."

" Wot about?" asked Squeaky, determined to delay as long as possible his entry into the tiger's cage.

" 'Ow do I know?" cried Hank, exasperated. " If you can't talk, listen. You might 'ear something."

" I shall 'ear a jugful all right," said Squeaky prophetically, resigned at last to his fate.

" Well, get on with it," said Hank, pushing him round the corner. " Don't 'ang about. Get in there while I start from the top. Go on."

Squeaky moved slowly towards the café entrance, muttering to himself: " Fancy meeting *you* 'ere. No. Fancy meetin' you *'ere* . . ."

His passing was not unobserved by the three inmates, and when at last he summoned up courage to enter, his opening speech died on his lips for, as far as he could see, the place was empty.

This suited Squeaky down to the ground. He was about to step smartly back into the street, when the door slammed behind him and he found himself cut off by Walrus.

" Come right in," invited the big Scandinavian genially, edging Squeaky away from the door.

" 'Ere, wot's the game?" said Squeaky, backing away nervously as Tub appeared from the stairway and Frank's ominous bulk rose from behind the counter.

Uncle Hank to the Rescue

" That's what *we'd* like to know," said Tub pleasantly.
" What do you want, Squeaky?"

Squeaky gulped. Tub's smiling eyes gave him the horrors.

" He vants to spy on us," said Walrus, reaching out and giving Squeaky's ear a playful tweak. " Don't you, Squeaky?"

"Why should I?" asked Squeaky feebly, dodging away.

" You don't know, by any chance, that we've got those kids upstairs?" suggested Tub, lounging against the counter and lighting a cigarette.

Squeaky made as if to speak, but no sound came. He was dumb with fright. Tub's next remark was addressed to Walrus.

" I think he's come just in time," he said thoughtfully. " He can help us."

" By yiminy, dat's a good idea," grinned Walrus.

Tub turned to Squeaky. " We've always been scared you and your pal might squeal. Now we're going to make sure that you won't." He paused effectively and blew a cloud of smoke up to the ceiling. " You're going to put those kids out of the way."

" *Me?*" exploded Squeaky, his eye popping out of his head with fright.

" Don't be alarmed," said Tub in a syrupy voice. " We've made all the arrangements. We're just waiting for the tide to turn."

" 'Ere, nark it," said Squeaky, shocked into speech at last. " That's murder."

" Yeah. That's what they'll charge you with," said Tub coolly. " That is, if you're silly enough to get caught."

" Blimey, I'm orf," muttered Squeaky, making a sudden plunge for the door.

"Not yet," said Tub lazily, while Squeaky wriggled helplessly in Walrus's embrace. He turned to the counter, where Frank was watching proceedings with a cold professional eye. "Give him a little drink, Frank. Might put some heart into him."

As Frank reached beneath the counter, Squeaky allowed himself to be propelled towards it. Whatever lay before him, a drink wouldn't come amiss.

．　．　．　．　．　．　．　．　．

Meanwhile, David and Dusty were struggling desperately to hoist Shelagh up to the attic skylight. Two rickety chairs and the mattress were all they could find to aid them, and at each attempt she failed by a few inches to reach the wooden beam.

"If only we had some rope," said David dismally, "we could make knots in it and throw it over the beam and then shin up it somehow."

"I know," agreed Dusty. "We must never start out on an adventure again without yards and yards of rope."

"Listen," said Shelagh. "What's that funny noise?"

The three children stood motionless. The noise seemed to come from the roof. They gazed up at the skylight. It was covered with dust and cobwebs, but through it, dimly, they could see a face, a large round blob of a face crowned with a Merchant Navy cap.

"It's—it's Uncle Hank!" shouted Dusty.

The face made cautionary grimaces and vanished.

A second later there was a sharp crack as the skylight, long disused, was prised up, and the face reappeared in the opening.

"Uncle Hank!" cried Dusty joyously. "However did you manage to find us?"

"Never mind that now," said Hank brusquely. "You

got to get outa here pronto. Hurry up, now. One at a time."

Once more Shelagh scrambled up on the tottering pile of chairs and mattress. But this time two strong arms reached down and swung her on to the beam. After that it was easy. In a few moments all three were crouched on the tiles.

"Now then, easy does it," said Hank, crawling backwards down the slope of the roof. "I got a ladder down be'ind that chimney stack on to a flat roof. Then we move the ladder, see, and get down to the ground."

. . . .

When Joe Stark reached the café five minutes later, a quick squint through the lace curtains told him that he must work fast if he wanted to get hold of Dusty and find out the number of the pump case. He hurried down the side passage and round to the back of the premises.

He was a bit surprised when he saw the ladder in place, but he climbed up nimbly, and very soon had swung himself through the skylight into the attic. Here again was disquieting evidence in the shape of a heap of old chairs and a mattress and no sign of any children, but almost instantly the sound of approaching voices and footsteps put an end to speculation.

Stark flattened himself against the wall on the hinge side of the door. Events were moving faster than he'd bargained for. Out of the tail of his eye he saw the little door panel slide back.

"Must be asleep round de corner," said the deep voice of Walrus.

The key turned in the lock and the door was flung open.

Stark reached out and gently pulled it towards him. Spare and lightly built, if it came to a fight, he was no match for Tub and Walrus, and he knew it, but what he lacked in strength he made up in cunning. Already a plan had formed in his mind. Calmly he waited for his adversaries to fall in with it.

Walrus was the first to enter. Tub and Squeaky remained on the landing.

"Show a leg, you kids," bellowed Walrus, with awful jocularity. "Ve're goin' to take you for a nice little trip down the river."

There was no response.

"Come on. You ain't deaf," shouted Tub, who was in no mood for trifling.

Walrus skirted the pile of furniture and peered round the corner.

"Holy mackerel! They ain't here, Tub."

"Cut out the funny business," said Tub roughly, from the doorway. "There's no time to waste."

"I'm tellin' you, they ain't *here*," repeated Walrus indignantly. "See for yourself."

Tub strode into the room. A string of oaths escaped him as he took in the open skylight and the tell-tale heap of furniture.

Joe Stark seized his chance with lightning speed. Stepping neatly round the door, he had closed and locked it before the other two had even realized his presence. Then with a rude gesture at the open panel, he dived down the stairs and hurried off to await developments in the side passage. Clearly, the attic would not hold Tub and Walrus for very long and, failing information from Dusty, those two were his only hope of picking up the trail of the jewels.

Tub and Walrus regarded each other in speechless wrath and amazement. Neither of them could believe that Squeaky had either the wit or the spirit to accomplish this swift turning of the tables. Yet who else could it have been?

Tub leapt to the door and applied his eyes to the spy hole.

"You lousy little blackleg! Open this door or it'll be the worse for you," he demanded furiously.

Squeaky, who had had a sufficient number of drinks to produce an overpowering desire for sleep, stood blinking stupidly in the gloom of the landing, trying to figure out how Joe Stark came to be in the attic from which the children, apparently, had been spirited away. Dimly envisaging the hand of Providence in league with Hank Miller, Squeaky shook his head.

"Now, listen," said Tub threateningly; "no doubt you think you've been very clever, but you'll regret this. Open the door at once."

A slow grin spread over Squeaky's face as it came to him that, for once, he had the upper hand. It was true that the situation was not of his contriving, but he relished it no less on that account.

"Open it yerself," he said, grinning defiantly. And, deftly flicking the little panel across the blazing eyes of Tub, Squeaky swaggered down the stairs, through the café, and out into the sunshine of a sultry afternoon.

As for Frank, it must be recorded that his capacity for not being surprised was put to some slight strain as first Joe Stark, who had certainly not entered by way of the street, and then Squeaky Watts, the one at a purposeful trot and the other with the air of a conqueror, left his premises without so much as a word.

When he could disregard it no longer, Frank yawned fit to split his tonsils, oozed off his stool, and slowly climbed the stairs to investigate the tumult which was issuing from his top story.

CHAPTER VIII

All Aboard for the Gas-works

Like many bachelor uncles, Hank Miller had discovered that you can never fail to please a young person by offering a meal away from home. As soon as he judged that they were out of danger, he led his three charges to a coffee-stall parked on a piece of waste land, sat them down on a nearby form, and provided them with cups of tea and buns.

"Now, get outside this lot," he said gruffly, "and then I'm goin' to take you 'ome."

The children sipped their tea and bit into the sticky buns with healthy enjoyment, and for some moments nobody spoke. Then David, after an exchange of meaning looks and nods with the other two, said: "Uncle Hank, it was jolly fine of you to rescue us like that, and we want to show you how much we appreciate it." He paused, and Hank grinned in an embarrassed sort of way. "We're the Silent Three," David went on, "and we're going to let you join."

"I'm goin' to do more than that, my boy," said Hank, the grin fading to an expression of glum foreboding. "I'm goin' to join a silent brother'ood of about three thousand, and serve me right."

David and Shelagh could make nothing of this, but Dusty, without fully understanding, perceived that his uncle was very far from joking.

"What three thousand, Uncle Hank?" he asked nervously.

Hank did not reply at once. When he did, his voice

was solemn and somehow humble, and he seemed to
have forgotten Dusty's question.

"Now, look 'ere," he said, gazing earnestly down at
the three young faces. "*I* started all this caper because
I carried something on board ship and didn't know what
it was. I was a fool, and it's led to nothing but a lot of
crimes that get worse and worse. And now you're all in
mortal danger and there's no gettin' away from it. Look
wot's just 'appened to you at that Dago's 'ole."

"But you got us out of it," David pointed out cheerfully.

"So I did," agreed Hank soberly; "but next time
p'raps I won't be able to. You kids know enough to put
those crooks where they belong, and they'll do their best
to stop you, see?"

Dusty, who had listened to his uncle with increasing
agitation, burst out: "But what are you going to do?"

"I'm goin' to see you all safely 'ome," said Hank,
squaring his shoulders and speaking with unshakable
determination, "and then I'm goin' to do wot I should
'ave done in the first place. I'm goin' to tell the police
all about them jewels and everything. That'll put paid
to the 'ole wretched business."

Dusty jumped to his feet. David and Shelagh looked
at him curiously.

"You mustn't, Uncle Hank," he begged, no longer
able to suppress his alarm. "You *mustn't* tell the police,
or *anybody*."

Touched by this passionate concern, Hank put a clumsy
arm round the boy's shoulder. "I shall get through it
all right, Dusty boy," he said comfortingly.

"But somebody else won't!" cried Dusty wildly,
breaking away from the encircling arm.

"Oh?" said Hank, beginning to see that Dusty had

more on his mind than solicitude for his uncle. "Who?"

Dusty opened his mouth to reply, and then closed it tightly. He had cornered himself. But he had to say something. The others were waiting.

"It's somebody very important, and I can't tell you who," he said stubbornly.

"But you can't have secrets from the Silent Three," objected David, nettled by this disregard of himself as leader.

"Yes, I can," said Dusty sullenly.

"It's against the rules," countered David hotly.

"This one isn't against the rules," argued Dusty, resolved at all costs to keep his secret.

"I don't know what all this is about," broke in Hank sternly, "but it don't alter *my* plans. And the sooner I get you 'ome, the better. Come along now."

Hank made a move in the direction of the tram terminus. The others followed slowly, dragging their feet disconsolately over the rough ground. Somehow, after all the perils and excitements of the last twenty-four hours, each of them felt it was very tame, not to say cowardly, to just give up and go home.

"*I'm* not going home," said David, stopping suddenly.

"What's that?" said Hank, turning.

"I said, I'm not going home," repeated David, facing up to him boldly. "We've set out to get those jewels and we're going to get them."

"That's right, David," said Shelagh.

"I want to go after them too, Uncle Hank," said Dusty urgently.

"Never say die, eh?" said Hank, his eyes twinkling. "Well, you're a game lot, I must say. But I can't let you run any more risks, even if we knew where they was. Come on 'ome now."

All Aboard for the Gas-works

Once more Hank began to move.

" But we *do* know, Uncle Hank," said Shelagh, eagerly clutching his arm. " They're in the gas-works. David followed them."

" Well, blow me down!" exclaimed Hank, flabbergasted. " D'you mean the gas-works just down the river?" he added, his surprise merging into interest.

" That's right," said David. " They put the crate in a stores building, and I heard a man say they're not going to open it yet."

" Why didn't you tell me that before?" demanded Hank. " I know them gas-works well." He paused and the children watched him expectantly. " If I got in from the river side," he went on, his enthusiasm growing as the ways and means suggested themselves, " I could make me way to the stores part easy." He paused again and gazed down at the children doubtfully. " But wot am I goin' to do with you kids? 'Tain't safe to leave you to go 'ome alone."

" We're coming too, of course," said David instantly.

Hank pulled his right ear with a horny hand and eyed them doubtfully.

" You *must* let us come, Uncle Hank," insisted Dusty.

" *Please*," begged Shelagh.

" Well, I can see it's no good tryin' to stop you," said Hank, with half-humorous resignation, " but you'll 'ave to be'ave yerselves and do as I say. Now, look 'ere," he went on seriously, " I know a tugmaster bloke wot runs down to collect coke barges. He'd take us aboard and you could wait there for me off the gas-works jetty."

" We'll see about that later," David put in truculently.

" Oh, don't start arguing, David!" cried Dusty. " If Uncle Hank gets that muffler with the jewels, *everybody's* safe."

The Bellamy Jewels

"I say, what about Mummy?" said Shelagh, whose conscience had suddenly begun to work. "She'll be worried to death."

"Can't we phone her and say we're all right? Look!" said David, pointing in the direction of the tram terminus, "there's a call-box over there."

"Now wait a minute," said Hank, "you'd better leave yer mother to me. If she sets the police to find you, we *are* in a mess. You wait 'ere."

No sooner was Hank out of earshot than David turned on Dusty.

"Now, what's all this secret?"

"I can't tell you," said Dusty doggedly.

"But you *must*," ordered David.

"I *can't*!" cried Dusty desperately. "It would upset you too much."

"I like that!"

"Oh, leave off, David," said Shelagh. "You're not to quarrel."

"Well, it isn't fair. He can't have secrets from the leader."

"Why not?" giggled Shelagh. "It's a secret society, isn't it? Anyway, here comes Uncle Hank. You can't quarrel in front of him."

Hank had the air of a man who has lately emerged from a testing ordeal, and not entirely with flying colours.

"What did Mummy say?" called Shelagh.

"Plenty," said Hank briefly.

"Did she say we could go?"

"Well—not exactly," admitted Hank, who had, in fact, quietly replaced the receiver while Mrs. Ford was still questioning him, "but she knows you're safe with me."

Satisfied with this, the three set off with Hank across the road.

All Aboard for the Gas-works

" Uncle Hank," said Dusty, as they turned down towards the river, " what are we going to do with the jewels when we've got them?"

Hank was in no two minds about this.

" I'm goin' to throw 'em into the nearest police station, and then I'm goin' to run like— like anything, before they see who done it."

Dusty said no more, but as they hurried along he supposed to himself that the police, just as well as Mr. Merryvale, could return the jewels to their owner. All the same, he was a bit worried.

Hank's friend the tugmaster was an easy-going old boy with a bristly grey beard and keen but kindly blue eyes sheltering beneath vast overhanging eyebrows. His name was Mr. Crabtree. He was fond of children and he readily agreed to take Hank and his charges as far as the gas-works in the tug *Daisy Belle*.

It was fun chugging down mid-stream in the sunshine, and at first the children, seated in the small deck cabin shelter, looked about them eagerly, the two Londoners pointing out places of interest. Then David said suddenly: " I say, we ought to make Uncle Hank a member of the Silent Three before we go any farther."

" Yes," agreed Dusty. " Shall we do it now?"

David nodded, and Dusty fetched Hank, who was gossiping with his friend at the wheel.

" You've got to be enrolled, Uncle Hank," David told him.

" Oh, 'ave I?" said Hank, smiling broadly.

" This is very serious, you know," said David disapprovingly.

Hank rearranged his features to a suitable gravity and David continued: " Now, you do everything we do."

Hank blundered obediently through the ritual and then

said, after David: " I swear my solemn oath not to tell
a soul and to follow my leader."

" That's me," added David.

" Ah, I thought it might be," remarked Hank drily.

David gave him a sharp look and then said formally:
" Accepted in the name of the Silent Four."

The ceremony ended with hand-shaking all round.
David said: " We're the Silent Four now, and we stick
together. Right?"

" Right," echoed Shelagh and Dusty.

" That's all very well," protested Hank, foreseeing
complications, " but I can't go trailin' all over the gas-
works with you three be'ind me. You'll 'ave to wait
aboard till I get back."

" Wait *aboard*!" said David indignantly.

" You won't 'ave to wait long," Hank assured him.
" I know every bit of them gas-works."

" I'll tell you what," offered David handsomely. " As
you know the place, you can take the lead when we get
ashore."

" You're a proper 'andful, you are," said Hank, gazing
at him with a mixture of respect and despair. " A nice
kind of a caper I've let meself in for. I dunno, I'm sure."

" Don't you worry, Uncle Hank," said Dusty confidently. " We'll take care of you."

" Look!" cried Shelagh, " we're pulling in to the shore.
That must be the gas-works."

She pointed to a huge, windowless brick building
situated well back from the river, with lesser buildings
grouped around it, some connected with the main building
by covered passage-ways, others standing alone. A narrow-
gauge railway was laid out for the conveyance of waste
products to barges moored alongside, and strings of
trucks, some empty, others loaded, awaited transport.

All Aboard for the Gas-works

The *Daisy Belle* drew slowly in towards the jetty, nosing her way among anchored lighters and barges breasting the outgoing tide. Farther down-stream, tied to the wharf, her polished brasses winking in the sun and her smart paintwork drawing the eye in the surrounding drabness, lay a fire float. Moored just below her, a trim motor speed-boat rocked gently on the waves of passing river traffic. The two boys eyed these craft enviously.

The *Daisy Belle* shut off steam and rode easily into her mooring. The sudden quiet was rent by the piercing scream of a steam whistle.

" What's that for, Uncle Hank?" shouted Shelagh, clapping her hands to her ears.

" Day shift goin' off," explained Hank. " It's a good time for us."

As the ear-splitting blast died down, crowds of workmen began to stream along the waterfront. Many were on foot, but a large number rode bicycles. The air was filled with shouts and ringing bells.

Hank stepped ashore and the three children followed him. Mr. Crabtree waved to them from his little bridge.

" Wot time're you goin' back, Sid?" called Hank.

Mr. Crabtree put his hand in his trousers pocket and pulled out a large silver watch, which he examined with a calculating eye.

" Five o'clock," he said, " and not a minute later."

" Okay. Might see you. Thanks for the ride."

Mr. Crabtree nodded genially and Hank turned away and led the children along the jetty towards the crowded wharf.

" Now then," he said, " we've got to keep out of sight. The best thing is to make our way round the retort dump, then through the retort houses. We'll 'ave to wait our chance."

. . . .

The Bellamy Jewels·

When Tub and Walrus got away from Frank's Café they hurried· to the nearest tram stop and boarded a tram going east. Stark gave them a few minutes' start before he nipped out of the side passage and followed them. They went on top of the tram because Tub needed urgently to think, and Tub couldn't think very well unless he had a cigarette in his mouth.

This was very convenient for Joe Stark, who popped in below and sat down on the far side of a fat woman in a plaid shawl with gold rings in her ears and a basket of clothes pegs on her lap. Stark wriggled himself well back into the seat, and took a threepenny ticket. He had no idea where he was going.

Up on top, Tub offered fourpence and said " Two to the gas-works, please." When the conductor had gone, the two men sat in silence for a while. Tub had plenty to think about and none of it was pleasant. The kids had escaped him once more, by whose aid he did not know, but he suspected Hank. That made four of them to outwit, even supposing they had not informed the police, not to mention Merryvale, whose continued silence was beginning to assume a sinister aspect.

Then there were the inquiries that were bound to have been started by the finding of Ginger Green's body. Suspicion would have been pointed at every man who had been on board the *Tilbury Pride* that night, and sooner or later it would catch up with him and Walrus. Unless he could seize the jewels and clear out within an hour or so, they were done for.

The tram swooped and swayed along. All the windows were shut, and it was hot and full of smoke. Walrus yawned several times in quick succession. He thought he felt hungry. He began to imagine what he would have for his next meal, but he soon discovered that the idea of eating food was distasteful. He yawned again and glanced at Tub.

"How far is it, dis gas-vorks?"

"Not far," said Tub absently.

"London is a big city. Full of gas-vorks," observed Walrus pensively. "How you know dis de right one?"

"Cos I use my eyes, that's why," snapped Tub. "Pump case is labelled Bickton Gasworks."

Walrus said no more but fell into an uneasy reverie concerning the movement of ships at sea and the movement of trams on land. He wished he was at sea. You could walk about in a ship and you had something to do. He rose with great promptness when Tub said "Here we are," and thankfully turned his back on the tram as it sailed away to its destination.

Stark, who had jumped off at the last moment, joined a queue of people at the tram stop and bided his time.

While Tub and Walrus stood debating the best way to enter the gas-works, the steam whistle sounded, and soon the workmen began to hurry through the main gates. Tub and Walrus crossed the road and worked their way through the crowd round to the waterfront.

Stark followed them as closely as he dared.

"How do we know where to start, Tub?" inquired Walrus, who was already beginning to feel better.

"Watch me," said Tub out of the side of his mouth.

He lounged casually up to a workman who had stopped in the shelter of a building to light his pipe.

"Which is the stores building, mate?"

Stark flattened himself against the wall round the corner to catch the reply.

"It's along over there," replied the man, indicating the direction with a flaming match. "Go down past these buildings and turn to the right."

" Thanks, pal," said Tub, as the man went on his
way. " We'll hang about a bit till the crowd's gone," he
added to Walrus. " No sense in getting folks suspicious."

Joe Stark watched them move slowly off. This was
his opportunity. He knew the general direction of the
stores building. He must get there first and he must
work like lightning.

By this time Hank and the children had reached the
entrance to a retort house.

" The stores are in a building on the other side," said
Hank in a penetrating whisper. " We'll get through 'ere.
But wait till I say so." He poked a cautious head round
the open doorway. " Now!"

At the same moment Tub and Walrus arrived outside
a door on which there was a notice-board reading
" STORES. No admittance. By Order."

Although the door was open, a jutting barrier of brick
wall prevented them from seing inside the building. They
edged cautiously through the doorway and listened.

" I can hear somebody working inside," whispered Tub.

" I'll lay 'em out," replied Walrus hoarsely, clenching
his fists.

" Don't be a fool," said Tub harshly. " We've got
enough on our plates as it is. Wait."

Joe Stark, slipping into the building by another door
on the far side, had had no difficulty in identifying the
pump case. It stood alone amid a welter of pipes and
valves; it bore the shipping marks of the Ixion S.S. Co.,
and there were unmistakable signs that it had already
been tampered with.

Stark seized a handy crowbar and got busy.

Behind him, arranged in tiers along the wall, were
rows of stock bins filled with rivets, nuts and bolts, and
a variety of small parts and tools.

All Aboard for the Gas-works

Stark worked with speed and skill, his eyes and ears constantly alert. There was a sharp crack as he prised the timber loose. He laid down the crowbar carefully and peered into the opening. Lying snugly just inside was a red-spotted muffler, its four corners knotted together. Stark's eyes gleamed. He lifted it out and took a swift peep inside. He whistled softly to himself as the priceless gems winked and sparkled back at him. Then he raised his head sharply. Heavy footsteps were advancing from the door by which he had entered.

Dropping the bundle into the nearest stock bin, Stark strolled casually forward, his hands in his trousers pockets, and an expression of mild inquiry on his foxy little face.

The newcomers, two burly workmen in oily dungarees, each balancing a heavy iron pipe on his shoulder, stared at him suspiciously.

" Wot are *you* doin' 'ere?" said the first, whose name was Bert, unshouldering his pipe and letting it fall to the ground with a thud.

" Er—I'm looking for the foreman," said Stark civilly. " Have you seen him?"

" No," said the other bluntly, " and you won't neither, in '*ere*."

" Sorry. Somebody told me I would," said Stark easily. He turned and made towards the brick barrier behind which Tub and Walrus were listening.

" You come out this way with us," ordered Bert firmly. " *We'll* show you where the foreman's office is."

Raging inwardly, Stark turned and retraced his steps. Charlie, the second workman, laid down his iron pipe and both stood aside for him to pass. He had no choice but to allow himself to be escorted from the building.

As their footsteps died away, Tub poked his head round the corner of the wall. Followed by Walrus, he crept stealthily forward. At sight of the gaping pump case, they both increased their pace. Tub fell upon the opening and frantically searched inside.

"Vhen you said somebody vas vorking," observed Walrus sarcastically, "you said a yugful."

"How was I to know?" said Tub, rounding on him furiously. "That blasted kid's at the bottom of this, I'll be bound."

Walrus shrugged his huge shoulders and gazed around him gloomily. Suddenly his eye was caught by the bright red of Squeaky's muffler nestling in the stock bin.

"Hey, Tub. Look!" he cried, snatching up the bundle and untying the knots with clumsy haste.

For a brief moment the two men gloated silently, then "Quick! Somebody coming!" said Tub tensely.

Three figures darkened the doorway at the end and came heavily towards them. Tub stepped in front of Walrus, who retied the knots with shaking hands and dropped the bundle back into the stock bin.

"'Ere, wot's goin' on 'ere to-day?" called Bert, who was accompanied by Charlie and a mechanic with a bag of tools. "Wot d'*you* blokes want?" he demanded aggressively, as they came to a standstill.

"We're off a tug and we're looking for the barge ganger," replied Tub glibly.

"Oh, *are* you," said Bert, looking him up and down. "First it was a man off a barge looking for the foreman. Now it's two men off a tug looking for the ganger." Bert paused, sucked his teeth deliberately, and turned to his mate. "Charlie, if we' ad anything in 'ere worth pinching, I should begin to wonder."

"Ve vouldn't pinch anything, mister," said Walrus, twisting his ugly face into what he believed to be a beguiling smile.

All Aboard for the Gas-works

Bert guffawed rudely.

"You look a proper bedtime story-teller, you do," he said. "If you want the ganger's office, it's this way."

Tub and Walrus exchanged glances. Walrus's blood was up and he was spoiling for a fight. But Tub's eyes told him no.

"Come on," said Bert impatiently. "We got work to do."

Tub moved forward and Walrus followed sullenly. A few moments later the key turned in the lock and Squeaky's red muffler, with its priceless contents, was left once more in the bin.

By this time Hank and his party had reached the door by which Tub and Walrus had entered. Hank motioned the children in and closed the door carefully. They crept round the brick wall and stood listening.

"Okay," said Hank. "This is the place. Now we must 'urry."

The pump case was soon discovered in all its yawning emptiness.

"Somebody's been 'ere before us," observed Hank grimly. The children gazed at him dumbly. Dusty's heart sank and all his fears for Captain Ford crowded back on him. With a tremendous effort he kept himself from bursting out with the story of his interview with Mr. Merryvale. "Well, that's that, I suppose," Hank went on, trying to speak cheerfully. "We done our best, but we wasn't quick enough."

"I wonder who it was," mused David, frowning.

"I dunno. There's quite a number o' people interested in them jewels. But we shan't find out by 'anging around 'ere," said Hank positively. "Come on now."

"Wait a minute," said David. "They might have left some clues. Let's have a look round."

"Well, 'urry up, then," said Hank grudgingly. "I don't fancy meself convincin' the management that I'm takin' you kids round the gas-works for fun."

The children scattered quickly while Hank watched and listened. It was Dusty who pounced on the red muffler.

"Here they are, Uncle Hank," he cried, holding it up joyfully.

The others crowded round him.

"Open it, Dusty. Let's have a look," said Shelagh excitedly.

"We can't stop starin' now," said Hank. "Give 'em to me and let's get away before anybody comes."

Dusty handed over the bundle.

"Now then," said Hank, when they got outside, "we 'aven't got much time. You three run on and see that Mr. Crabtree don't go off without us. I got a bone in me leg."

.　.　.　.　.　.　.　.　.　.

Joe Stark, having been escorted by Bert and Charlie into the presence of the stores foreman, had quickly invented a message regarding iron pipes from a well-known firm which, as it happened, was due to make a delivery.

The foreman was just packing up to go home. He had promised to take his wife to the pictures and the message caused him considerable annoyance. Muttering explosively, he reached at once for his telephone.

"Okay for me to go?" said Stark, making towards the door.

"Yes, yes," said the foreman testily. "Get out of my sight. You've ruined my evening." He rattled the telephone savagely. "Hullo! Hullo!"

Stark slipped out, closed the door, and took a quick look round. There was no sign of Bert and Charlie, nor yet of Tub and Walrus. But to get back directly to the stores building he must cross a large open space and his object would be plain to anybody who might be interested. Stark decided on a roundabout route.

Taking cover from sheds and buildings and dodging out of sight behind trucks and refuse dumps, he arrived some five minutes later at the locked door. It was a stout door, and it was clearly useless to try to force it. The window alongside was protected by wire netting. Stark set off round the back of the building in search of another entrance.

Turning a corner cautiously, he saw Hank and the children emerge. Their backs were towards him and they were headed for the waterfront. Stark's eyes darkened as he saw that Hank was carrying the red spotted muffler.

Suddenly the children ran off towards the river with Hank following at a smart amble. He was getting on, was Uncle Hank, and his heart was not what it used to be, which was perhaps the reason why he doubled up so quickly when Stark leapt on him from the rear. It was a very brief struggle, and it ended, alas, with Hank lying unconscious on the cobble-stones and Stark in possession of the muffler full of jewels.

. . . .

The barge ganger's office turned out to be in a corrugated iron shed down by the water. On a notice-board outside was pinned a sheet of paper which read " Hands Wanted. Apply within."

Inside, the barge ganger himself sat behind a trestle table drinking a mug of tea. He was a formidable-looking fellow with a cauliflower ear and a broken nose, and he was not to be trifled with. His name was Stanley Briggs, at one time known in boxing circles as Battling Briggs of Bermondsey. A sense of humour was not his strong point, and his workmates took a delight in pulling his leg.

" 'Ere you are, Stan," said Bert, poking his head round the door. " Coupla chaps want to sign on."

" Ah," said Stan, putting down his mug and wiping a hairy hand across his mouth. " Bring 'em in. Could do with 'em."

Bert stood aside and watched with an artful smile while Tub and Walrus entered. Bert rather prided himself on being a judge of character, and he reckoned he'd got the measure of Tub and Walrus. He hung around the doorway, sucking his teeth expectantly.

" Name?" said Stan, picking up a pencil and drawing an old exercise book towards him.

" Jackson," said Tub unhesitatingly, " Thomas Jackson. My mate's name is Hanson."

Stan wrote down the names in a round laborious hand.

" Got yer cards?"

Tub made a show of going through his pockets. Walrus did likewise.

" Sorry," said Tub carelessly. " Must have left them in my other jacket."

Stan threw down his pencil and rose to his feet angrily. " Wot's the game, comin' in 'ere and wastin' my time? D'you want a job, or don't you?"

" Ask him," said Tub off-handedly, jerking a thumb over his shoulder at Bert, who was grinning in the background. " It was his idea."

" I see," said Stan heavily, moving slowly round the table and fixing Bert with a murderous glare. " Another of your little jokes, I suppose. Very laughable, I'm sure. Well, this time you ain't goin' to get away with it!"

Shoving Tub and Walrus aside, Stan made a dive for Bert, who turned and fled. He knew better than to try conclusions with Battling Briggs.

All Aboard for the Gas-works

" I'll learn yer!" roared Stan, charging across the open like a bull in a field.

As they disappeared from sight, Walrus said admiringly: " Is good, Tub. Now ve go back for the jewels, yaas?"

.   .   .   .

When the children reached the jetty the tug *Daisy Belle* was still lying alongside, but there was no sign of Mr. Crabtree.

" Well, anyway, he hasn't gone without us," said Shelagh thankfully. " I say, wasn't it lucky finding the jewels like that?"

" Yes," said Dusty uneasily, " but I wish Uncle Hank would hurry up. I hope nothing's happened to him."

" Perhaps he's gone to a police station, like he said," suggested Shelagh.

" Look!" said David, pointing to a running figure. " There's Merryvale's man Stark. I wonder what he's doing here."

" Gosh! He's got the jewels!" cried Dusty. " I can see the red muffler. He's making for the river."

" And there's Tub and Walrus after him!" cried David, as two more figures came pelting across the open. " Come on, Silent Four. Follow me!"

Stark reached the water's edge just below the fire float. Tub and Walrus were less than a hundred yards behind him. At his feet lay the small speed-boat. Breathing fast, Start untied the painter, jumped in and started up the engine. With a cough and a splutter she sprang to life and sped rapidly away from the wharf, making a course up-stream.

" This way," yelled Tub to Walrus. " We'll board the fire float and get after him."

The fire float was a larger and more powerful craft

with the lines of a small cabin cruiser. Her substantial poop, raised above a narrow deck, carried her fire-fighting appliances and coils of hose. She was made fast to the wharf at bow and stern. While Walrus untied her, Tub leapt aboard and ran forward to the engine-room cabin. There was a swirl of water beneath her stern and the engine began to turn over sweetly and strongly. Walrus threw the bow painter on board and climbed down into the cabin beside Tub.

" Come on, Silent Four," panted David, pulling up abreast of the stern. " All aboard."

Shelagh and Dusty scrambled on to the narrow deck and David leapt after them. The fire float swung out into the stream and made off after the vanishing speed-boat.

CHAPTER IX

Uncle Hank Comes Clean

As the fire float gathered speed and the gas-works were left behind, the three children, crouched down in the stern clinging to the rails, eyed each other with more than a little misgiving. In the excitement of the moment David, fearless and single-minded, had seen only that the jewels were disappearing once more and had given chase without a thought of the consequence. Shelagh and Dusty had followed unhesitatingly. Now it was becoming clear to all three that they had put themselves at the mercy of two desperate men, and that it could only be a matter of minutes before they were discovered.

" What are we going to do now, David?" whispered Shelagh anxiously.

Uncle Hank Comes Clean

" Well . . . I don't quite know," confessed David,
" but I read somewhere that the best means of defence
is attack."

" Yes, but what with?"

" We'll find something," said David, looking about
him cautiously. " There's a boat-hook, for a start." He
crept forward and slid the long-handled implement
towards him.

" What about the hoses?" said Dusty thoughtfully.

" Golly! That would be wizard. I wonder how they
work?"

" I should think that wheel by the nozzle has something to do with it. Let's try."

Dusty rose up on his knees and peered round a coil
of hose lying on the poop just above him. Tub and
Walrus had eyes for nothing but Stark and the speed-
boat ahead. Slowly and carefully, with Shelagh's help,
Dusty uncoiled a few yards of hose while David kept
watch with the boat-hook. The hose was heavy and
unwieldy and their hearts were in their mouths in case
the weighty brass nozzle should slide overboard. But at
last they had a fair length to play with and the nozzle
firmly grasped between them, pointing forward at the
unconscious backs of Tub and Walrus.

" Shall we have a go?" said Dusty, his eyes glinting
with excitement.

" Okay."

Dusty gave a slow turn to the wheel on the side of the
nozzle. At first nothing seemed to happen. He turned
it farther and, as the water started to flow, the hose began
to slither and slide like a live thing. A dribble of water
came.

" Faster! Faster!" urged David.

Dusty gave the wheel two or three turns and the hose

leapt in their arms so that they could hardly keep their balance. A tremendous jet of water shot into the air and landed in the river over the bows.

Tub and Walrus turned as one man.

"Great suffering cats!" yelled Tub. "It's those blasted kids again. Here, take the wheel."

Tub leapt from the little cabin up on to the deck. At the same instant Dusty lowered the nozzle and the full force of the jet of water hit him squarely in the chest. Tub staggered and dodged wildly to one side, gasping for breath.

"Quick, Dusty! Give him another shot," shouted David, throwing down the boat-hook.

Between them the three children once more aimed their cumbrous weapon, and Tub received in his face the short-range impact of several tons of water. Helpless and blinded, he thrashed about, the relentless torrent forcing him ever closer to the boat's edge. Suddenly he lost his footing. With a shout of rage and a frantic waving of the arms, he plunged backward into the stream, and in a few moments his head was seen bobbing far astern.

"Oh gosh, I hope he can swim!" cried Shelagh.

"Never mind him," said David callously. "We've got to get rid of Walrus before we *all* get drowned."

Walrus was now in a horrible dilemma. He had lost his leader and he was not one to act on his own. He was no engineer. And, finally, he had three ruthless children on his hands. When the first volley of water struck him amidships, Walrus decided that, as far as he was concerned, the game was up. He battled his way out of the cabin and, without shame or ceremony, took a header overboard and, like the mammal whose name he bore, wallowed composedly shorewards. Even Shelagh could see that she need waste no concern for his welfare, and, indeed, their own safety was becoming a matter for instant action.

"You two take charge of the hose," ordered David, scrambling forward to the controls. "I know a bit about engines. I bet I can run this one all right."

Dusty and Shelagh turned off the hose and stood by. In the distance the speed-boat was drawing off rapidly.

"Oh, David, he's getting away!" cried Shelagh. "Hurry, hurry!"

"I'm doing the best I can," shouted David, frantically scanning dials and turning switches.

"See if you can help, Dusty," said Shelagh. "I'll keep watch."

Dusty joined David. His knowledge of combustion engines was even sketchier than David's, but he pointed to a lever.

"Try this one."

David pulled it towards him. With a roar the boat shot forward at full speed.

"Now we're off!" he yelled exultantly. "Man the hose for a broadside on the enemy."

The craft cut through the water at breakneck speed. Passing tugs and steamers hooted with alarm as David, defying all the rules of the river, swept down upon his quarry. The speed-boat was going all out, but it was no match in power.

"Ahoy, there!" yelled David, as they drew abreast. "Let him have it!"

Shelagh and Dusty took aim and let loose a torrential volley. Stark staggered, but held to his course.

"Keep it up! I'm going to circle round him."

David cut across the bows of the speed-boat. Stark swerved violently to the shore. By inches the two craft avoided collision and, as the fire float came about, another deluge swept the speed-boat from bow to stern. Her engine coughed and spluttered. She was finished. As David circled in mid-stream to return to the attack, Stark dived overboard and swam strongly for the bank. Before they could intercept him he had reached a small jetty and climbed ashore.

"We'll never catch him now," wailed Shelagh, as Stark shook himself like a wet terrier and ran off.

"I guess not," agreed David, bringing the fire float round in a curve towards the jetty. "The thing is, how do I stop this darned engine?"

"What about this thing?" said Dusty practically. "It's marked OFF. Try it."

David turned a switch on the dashboard. The engine stopped and the craft slid easily through the water and bumped alongside the jetty. The three children sprang out and made her fast.

The jetty belonged to a brewery, and at this hour work had ceased. The wharf was deserted.

"Where are we?" said Dusty, looking round.

"Well, there's the Tower of London," replied Shelagh, pointing across the river. "How do we get home from here, David?"

"Who said anything about going home? We've got to think out a plan. Besides, we've got to find out what's happened to Uncle Hank."

"I say," interrupted Dusty, as an idea occurred to him. "Stark works for Mr. Merryvale, doesn't he?"

"Yes, of course. But where does that get us?"

"It means that Stark is working *against* Mr. Merryvale," explained Dusty, pursuing his train of thought.

David and Shelagh exchanged bewildered glances.

"What on earth are you talking about?"

"Don't you see?" cried Dusty impatiently. "If Mr

Uncle Hank Comes Clean

Merryvale gets hold of the jewels, he'll be able to save your father."

" Save our *father*," repeated Shelagh. " What from?"

" Prison," said Dusty, who was so taken up with his own reasoning that he had completely lost sight of its meaning for Shelagh and David.

" Have you gone potty?" said David indignantly. " What on earth has Daddy got to do with it?"

Dusty's face turned red. He could think of nothing to say.

" Perhaps he's a bit mixed," put in Shelagh, the peace-maker.

" He'd better be," said David angrily. " There's going to be trouble if he starts talking about Daddy going to prison."

" You mean, save Uncle Hank, don't you, Dusty?"

" Yes, that's it," said Dusty, eagerly seizing the chance to cover his mistake. " If we go to Mr. Merryvale and tell him about Stark," he went on rapidly, " he'll be able to get the jewels and save Uncle Hank."

" All right," said David, pacified. " Let's go to Merry-vale's office, then."

. . . .

When Hank Miller came to himself he had a large bump on the back of his head and a shocking headache. It was some moments before he could collect his thoughts sufficiently to realize what had happened. He reached for his cap, put it on with a painful grimace and struggled to his feet. Suddenly it all came back to him. Stark had made off with the jewels and Heaven alone knew what had happened to the children. He hurried down to the jetty. No sign of them there. No sign, either, of Mr. Crabtree or the *Daisy Belle*.

The Bellamy Jewels

" I never should 'ave give way to 'em," Hank told himself severely. " I should 'ave took 'em 'ome in the first place."

He stood uncertainly by the water's edge. Was it a job for the police, or had he better go and make a clean breast of it to the captain?

Half an hour later he rang the bell at Number 49, Beverley Road. The door was opened by Captain Ford himself.

" What is it, Miller?"

" 'Ave the children got 'ome, sir?"

" No. They haven't."

Hank's face fell. The captain gave him a searching glance.

" Come in."

Hank grabbed off his cap, stifling a groan as he did so, and followed the captain into the living-room.

" Now then, Miller, what's wrong? Where are the children?"

" I left them at the gas-works, sir."

" Left them *where*?" said the captain blankly.

" At the gas-works, sir," repeated Hank miserably.

" What on earth were you doing there?"

" We were after the jewels, sir."

The captain stared. " I suppose you haven't been drinking, Miller?" he said sternly.

" No, sir."

" Do you feel well?"

" I know what you're thinking, sir," said Hank doggedly, " but it's the jewels that were aboard the *Tilbury Pride*."

" Good heavens, Miller! D'you mean to say those jewels were aboard my ship after all?"

" Yes, sir. And I carried them aboard, under false

pretences," said Hank, determined to go through with his confession, no matter what the cost to himself.

" And did you keep *silent* about it under false pretences?" said the captain angrily.

· " There's more in it than all that, sir," said Hank grimly. " There's a lot of crooks and murderers we got mixed up with—me and Squeaky. A couple of fools we was. But that ain't the point. There's higher-up men than us in it, and they're using your vessel and others besides. It's smugglin', sir, that's their racket. Smugglin' stolen jewels."

" Who do you mean, Miller?"

" That there Merryvale, sir. He's the 'ead crook of all the lot."

The captain was dumbfounded. ·

" *Merryvale?*"

" Yes, sir. Merryvale. Him and that Stark. Stark was at the gas-works and 'e's got the jewels. 'E's takin' 'em to Merryvale."

The captain was silent for a moment. This was a very serious matter, and it demanded instant action, but there must be no mistake.

" I suppose you really do mean all this, Miller?"

" Do I?" exclaimed Hank vengefully. " That Merryvale and Co. 'ave been at it for I dunno 'ow long, usin' ordinary seamen to do their dirty work and deceivin' people like you wot try to run decent ships."

" This is monstrous!" said the captain, now thoroughly roused. " I must go down and see Merryvale at once. But there's one more thing I'd like to know," he added as he moved to the door. " How does it come about that my children are mixed up in all this?"

" Well, sir," said Hank apologetically, " I'm afraid it's that nephew of mine. While 'e was 'idin' aboard ship 'e overheard a lot of talk, and I suppose 'e passed it on, and nothin' would do but they must all join in. That Master David, 'e's a fair caution," he added reminiscently. "There's no 'oldin' 'im, sir."

"I see," said the captain, not unpleased by this description of his son and heir. "Well, the sooner we find out what they're up to now, the better."

As the captain strode out into the hall, Mrs. Ford came along the passage from the kitchen.

"What's the matter, Jim? Where are you going?" she asked as the captain picked up his hat. And then, rather coldly: "Good evening, Mr. Miller."

"Oh, Mary, I've got to go down to the office."

"Is something wrong?" asked Mrs. Ford, scenting trouble. "Is it the children?"

"No, they're all right," said the captain quickly. "It's this jewel business. I want you to call Inspector White at Scotland Yard and ask him to come to Merryvale's office immediately. Tell him it's very urgent."

"But——" began Mrs. Ford.

"Now, don't worry," said the captain, kissing her hurriedly. "I won't be long. Come on, Miller."

. . . .

In Merryvale's office, his clothes still dripping with river water, Stark had just finished the story of his capture of the jewels which lay in a sodden bundle on Merryvale's desk.

"Good," said Merryvale, rubbing his hands together with pleasure. "Now we're all set."

"Have you fixed up a getaway?"

"I have. The *Seaspray* is waiting for us off Gravesend with steam up. But first I must collect a few things to take with me, and we'll burn the rest. I have a notion," he added thoughtfully, "that this office has not seen the last of Detective-Inspector White."

Uncle Hank Comes Clean

" Okay. I'd better look through my stuff too."

Stark disappeared into the inner room and Merryvale began to ransack the drawers of his desk. Absorbed in his task, he started uncomfortably when a sudden knock sounded on the outer door.

" Who is it?" he called sharply. " I'm busy."

" It's me, sir," came the answer in a boy's voice. " Dusty Bates."

Merryvale took a quick look round, dropped the bundle of jewels into the wastepaper basket, then stepped to the door and opened it.

On the landing stood Dusty, with Shelagh and David behind him.

" Come inside," said Merryvale, smiling suavely.

The three children crowded in. Merryvale closed the door, deftly turned the key, and slipped it into his pocket.

" It's about—about—what we were talking about, sir," said Dusty breathlessly. " You know—about the jewels and how you'd save Captain Ford."

" You leave Dad's name out of it," said David, butting in angrily.

Merryvale looked from one to the other, his eyebrows raised sardonically.

" Dusty's excited," explained Shelagh protectively. " He doesn't mean Daddy; he means Uncle Hank."

" Yes, that's it," agreed Dusty hastily. " And we've come to warn you that your man Stark is double-crossing you. He's got the jewels. We chased him in a fire float right up the river, but he got away from us."

" Indeed?" said Merryvale evenly. Then, raising his voice he called, " Stark!"

" That's him, Mr. Merryvale!" cried Dusty as Stark appeared grinning in the doorway. " He's got them. He took the jewels!"

" You're quite right, Dusty," said Merryvale calmly. " The jewels are here. Mr. Stark brought them back."

Dusty stared, his spirit suddenly dashed.

" But—is he working *with* you, then?"

"*Am* I?" said Stark, with an ugly guffaw. He turned to Merryvale, coarsely familiar. " Are we working together? I ask you?"

" I don't understand all this," said Dusty, baffled and bewildered.

" I do," said David bitterly. " They're both crooks."

" Hold your tongue, you little fool," snapped Stark.

" We're not afraid of you!" cried David, leaping to the outer door. " Come on, Silent Four. Follow me!"

He struggled fiercely with the door handle, but it was no use.

" Such charming children!" said Merryvale, surveying their defiant faces mockingly. " *So* intelligent. But unfortunately you talk too much." He moved to shepherd them towards the inner office. " And so we're going to put you where you'll be out of the way for a few hours."

" That's what you think!" cried David, charging at him, head down, while Dusty grappled with Stark.

" Now, don't let's be rough," said Merryvale pleasantly, stepping side with surprising agility and seizing David firmly from behind. " And you won't need that chair, young woman," he added to Shelagh. " You'll find it's quite comfortable in the other room."

" All right," said David, seeing that it was useless to resist. " But you wait till my father hears about this."

" Unfortunately I shall not be here," said Merryvale courteously. " Now, do make yourselves at home," he went on as he closed and locked the door on them. " I'm sorry I can't provide you with any refreshments, but I'm a little pressed for time."

Uncle Hank Comes Clean

"Blackfriars!" shouted the captain, striding across the road with Hank close behind.

Ernie shook his head and turned down the corners of his mouth. "Sorry, guv'nor. Got a date up west."

"Now, look here," said the captain, firmly grasping the handle of the door, "you've got no fare and my business is urgent. In fact," he added significantly, "it's concerned with Scotland Yard. Double fare if you hurry."

"Okay. Jump in," said Ernie, less impressed by Scotland Yard than by the promise of double fare. "Wot's the address?"

* * * * * * * *

In Merryvale's office there was now a scene of considerable chaos. Piles of papers were strewn all over the desk and the floor. A roaring fire was burning in the grate, which faced the desk and the window, and Stark was still ferreting about in the drawers of a filing cabinet like a dog at a dustbin.

"Aren't you nearly finished there, Stark?" said Merryvale impatiently, retrieving the bundle of jewels from the wastepaper basket and placing them on the desk.

"One more drawerful."

Merryvale looked at his wrist-watch. "We must leave here in five minutes. Hullo, who can this be?"

There was a loud knocking at the door. Both men stood motionless.

"Who is it?" called Merryvale peremptorily.

"Timkins."

"H'm," said Merryvale, running a coolly humorous eye round his disordered apartment. "I don't think they'd better come in here. They might get a hint of our plans." He paused briefly. "I'll see them in the corridor. Get the rest of this stuff burned and then slip downstairs with the jewels while I keep them talking. I'll join you in the yard outside."

Merryvale took the key from his pocket, unlocked the door, and contrived to get outside without allowing his visitors more than the barest glimpse of the interior.

"Ah, Timkins," he said affably, taking Tub's arm and drawing him down the corridor.

"Now look here, Merryvale," began Tub aggressively, "you know what we've come for."

Tub was pretty desperate by now, but he was not beaten yet. Money was what he needed. Money to buy a change of clothing; money to buy their way out of the country.

"But, my dear fellow, what's happened?" exclaimed Merryvale, with exaggerated concern. "You're soaking wet!"

"Never mind that," barked Tub, brushing the smooth plump hand away. "Stark has got the jewels and we want our cut—*now*. Otherwise——"

"Of course, of course," Merryvale intervened soothingly. "But let's get along to the caretaker's room. There's a fire there and you can both get dry while we talk."

.   .   .   .

When Dusty reached the window of Merryvale's office, he thought at first that the room was empty. Then he perceived that Stark was on his knees before the grate with his back to the window, rapidly tearing up papers and heaping them on to the fire which was roaring up the chimney. He also observed the bundle of jewels lying on Merryvale's desk. His eyes gleamed. Turning his head cautiously, he beckoned to David. While he waited, he took careful stock of the room and its contents.

"If we can get this window open and climb in," he

whispered, when David joined him, " we might be able to overpower him. See that sweater on the back of that chair ?"

David nodded.

" My idea is to creep up behind him and throw that over his head. He'll never hear us with Shelagh making all that row. Then, while he's struggling, we can bag the jewels and go back the way we came."

David nodded again, and between them they set to work on the window. Luckily Mr. Merryvale was not averse to fresh air, and the lower sash slid up easily and silently. Dusty lowered himself softly inside, reached out and picked up the sweater. David followed. Shelagh was putting up a wonderful performance on the inner door, kicking, hammering with her fists, and shouting for help. Creeping one on each side of the desk, they approached the kneeling figure of Stark.

There was a muffled bellow as the thick folds of the seaman's jersey enveloped his head. Stark rolled over on his back, his legs thrashing wildly. David instantly sat on his chest, wound the sleeves round his neck and tied them tightly, while Dusty ran to the desk, undid the bundle of jewels, and began stuffing them rapidly into his pockets.

Taken by surprise, Stark was momentarily at a disadvantage, but he was an active young man, and it was all David could do to keep him down. Loose papers flew about the room and into the grate, and the flames reached out avidly.

" Hurry up," mouthed David. " I can't hold him much longer."

Dusty, his pockets now bulging with treasure, swept all the papers from Merryvale's desk, filled the muffler with a variety of small objects lying beneath, retied it, and signalled to David. Less than five minutes from the time they set out, the boys were back in the inner office.

Stark blundered to his feet and tore off the suffocating jersey. The room was empty. His first thought was for the jewels. There lay the bundle, safe and sound. He grabbed it, thrust it inside his jacket, picked up his hat and made for the door. As he opened it, the draught from the open window set a further scurry of papers fluttering into the fireplace. Stark closed the door hurriedly and, setting his hat at a rakish angle, advanced warily towards the stairhead as Merryvale, with Tub and Walrus, emerged from a room at the end of the corridor.

"Ah, Stark," said Merryvale genially. "Have you finished off that little job for me?"

"Yes, gu'vnor. We're all set," replied Stark, with a meaning look.

"Splendid." Then, turning to Tub and Walrus: "Well, that's settled, then. You come here to my office at ten o'clock to-morrow morning and, if I'm not mistaken, you'll get quite a surprise at what's waiting for you. You leave it all to me."

Tub eyed him malignantly. Merryvale was a smooth customer, if ever there was one. A nice yarn he'd spun. Tub wouldn't trust him as far as he could throw him, but he had the whip hand now.

"Okay," he snarled. "But mind, no monkey business."

"My dear Tub, what a suggestion!" said Merryvale reproachfully. "And now you really must excuse me. I have a most urgent appointment. Come along, Stark, or we shall miss the bus."

At that moment Ernie Wilks drew up with a flourish at the street door.

The captain was better than his word, and Ernie was

Uncle Hank Comes Clean

contemplating a ten-shilling note with some satisfaction when two police cars swept in ahead of him and disgorged six policemen and a plain-clothes man.

"Thanks for your message, Ford," said the inspector, hurrying up to the captain. "I'm hoping to make a pretty big haul. There's a capital charge against two of your men, Timkins and Olsen, for the murder of Ginger Green. My lads have already tailed them here. Clayton and Spencer," he went on rapidly, the captain appearing to be struck dumb by this piece of news, "guard the street entrance. Allow nobody to leave. Sergeant, take one man and get round to the back premises. Miniver, patrol the building and keep your eyes skinned. Trubshaw, come with me."

As Inspector White hurried in with the astounded captain and Hank Miller, Ernie looked at his watch. It was early yet, and there might be something worth seeing. Turning his cab skilfully in the narrow street, he parked himself on the far side, produced half a cigarette from behind his left ear, and settled down to wait.

. . . .

Shelagh was thrilled by the story the boys had to tell on their return, and insisted on having a look at the jewels which had lured them on to so many adventures. When her squeals of wonder had died down and the jewels were safely back in Dusty's pockets, all three began to feel the call of home.

"I'm hungry," declared Shelagh.

"So'm I," said Dusty. "I wonder if they've gone yet."

"I'll slip along and see," said David.

"No, it's too dangerous," said Shelagh quickly. "They may still be there. After all, we have the jewels and we don't want to bump into them again. Let's give them a bit longer."

David raised his head and sniffed.

"What's that smell?"

"It's like something burning," said Dusty.

"Oh, look!" cried Shelagh. "Smoke's coming under the door. Oh, Dusty, do you think they've set the place on fire?"

"Gosh! All that paper on the floor! The flames must have spread into the room, and it's our only way out!" Dusty rushed to the window and climbed out on to the ledge. "I'm going to see if I can get through and unlock the door. You two start shouting. Maybe somebody in the street will hear you."

. . . .

When Merryvale turned the last corner of the stairs and saw Captain Ford, Inspector White, Hank Miller, and a uniformed police officer, he paused for a fraction of a second. Close on his heels was Stark, and behind him again were Tub and Walrus. If it came to force, they were equally matched. But Merryvale disliked any form of physical violence; he preferred to fight with words.

"Good evening, gentlemen," he called, hurrying down the remaining stairs. "Do you want to see me? I'm afraid I'm already late for an appointment. Stark," he added over his shoulder, "go ahead and see if you can find a cab."

"Not so fast," said Inspector White, stepping forward. "There's a little matter of some stolen jewellery to be cleared up first."

"In that case, Inspector," said Merryvale, as Stark slipped past him and ran for the door, "I think I can help you. For a start, I would recommend you to have a talk with these two gentlemen," indicating Tub and Walrus, who had vaulted the balustrade and made a headlong dash for the rear exit.

Uncle Hank Comes Clean

"I have that in mind also," replied Inspector White calmly. "In the meantime, Trubshaw, just run over Mr. Merryvale, will you? Sergeant Williams and his men will take care of the others."

"I must say you think of everything," bluffed Merryvale, submitting to the search with apparent good grace. "Just like the movies, isn't it? But you're wasting your time, you know."

"Cut the cackle," advised Trubshaw, as from front and back entrances there entered Stark, Tub and Walrus, each handcuffed to an officer, with an extra man in attendance.

"Find anything?" said Inspector White, addressing Stark's guardian.

"Only this, sir," said the officer, holding up Squeaky's red-spotted muffler. "Seems to be full of paper clips, rubber stamps, ink bottles, and other office gear."

"Dear me," said the inspector drily, his eyes alert for the effect of this announcement.

Stark turned a blank face to Merryvale, whose raised eyebrows momentarily betrayed him. Tub and Walrus glared ferociously at Merryvale, and Hank's expression was one of complete bewilderment.

"Before you go, Inspector," broke in Captain Ford urgently, "I must find out if any of these men have seen my two children and young Dusty Bates in the last hour or so."

"Merryvale?" queried the inspector.

"I've been in my office all the afternoon," replied Merryvale indifferently. "How should I know what they're up to?"

"Either of you two seen them?" said the inspector, turning to Tub and Walrus.

Tub shook his head. When last seen by him they had

been careering up-river in command of a fire float. For all he knew, they might all be drowned by now, and a good job too. He'd have his work cut out to account for the movements of himself and Walrus that afternoon, without tying himself up with any wretched kids.

"You'll excuse me buttin' in," said an apologetic voice from the street door, "but I 'ave an idea this 'ere buildin's on fire. And wot's more," added Ernie Wilks, "if it's kids you're lookin' for, there's a bunch of 'em on the top floor yellin' their bloomin' 'eads orf!"

When all the commotion had died down and the fire brigade had the blaze under control, Captain Ford gathered the children round him and signalled to Ernie Wilks to start up his taxi.

"Well, good-bye, Inspector," he said, holding out his hand. "Not a bad haul for you. Pity you didn't get the jewels as well."

"Oh, but we *did*!" cried Dusty, who had been so enthralled by the activities of the firemen that he had forgotten all about the contents of his bulging pockets. "Look!"

．　　．　　．　　．　　．　　．　　．　　．　　．

And what happened to Dusty?
With the aid of Captain Ford and a cheque for a thousand pounds from the company which had insured the Bellamy jewels, he was able to take up the career he had set his heart on. He became a cadet in the training ship *Conway*, and his foster parents in Hull never saw him again. He spent all his holidays with the Ford family, where Uncle Hank was always a welcome visitor, and they often talked together of the adventures of the Silent Four in the Quest of the Bellamy Jewels.

PRINTED IN ROMANIA

Abbey